WIFE FOR NOW

USA TODAY Bestselling Author
PENNY WYLDER

CHAPTER ONE

I sigh and check the clock on the wall.

Or at least, that's what I pretend I'm

doing. In reality, I'm checking through

the large floor-to-ceiling office

windows beside my desk, out of the

corner of my eye. Luke is still in there,

as usual. And as usual, he's bent over

his computer like a hunchback. That

man is going to give himself back

problems soon if I don't step in.

That's all I'm doing, I insist. Being

a good assistant. Helping out. Making

sure he doesn't need me to book

another chiropractor session in a

week's time.

This definitely isn't an excuse to

pop my head into his office for the

dozenth time today. Nope. Not an

excuse to stand near him and catch

the scent of his cologne; the smoky,

spicy scent that haunts my dreams.

Not a thinly veiled reason to stand near him and hope he hands me some more paperwork, just for that split second when our fingertips brush and my whole body goes electric.

"Luke?" I tap on his doorframe.

He glances up and flashes me one of his trademark Luke Rossfield smiles. I swear, in a past life the guy must have been some kind of Nordic god or something. Tall, blond and angular, he's got the kind of blue eyes that pierce right through you, and the cheekbones to finish the job. But when he smiles, it all softens, like he's sharing a secret. A little hint of emotion meant just for you. "Celia."

Not to mention the way my name melts on his tongue...

"Don't make me call Dr. Morgen on you again." I point at his spine.

Dutifully, he straightens, though the smile never leaves his lips. He arches his back and reaches up to rub the back of his neck with one hand.

"Old habits die hard. At least that

explains this crick in my neck." His

smile widens. "Thank you, Celia. What

would I do without you?"

My heart skips a beat. I force

myself to ignore it. "Probably slip a

disc," I respond. He laughs, and I take

that as my cue to spin back to my

chair. Just a few feet away, and yet,

with the glass of his office between us,

it feels like a million miles.

His phone starts to ring, and through the window, he catches my gaze just to roll his eyes dramatically. I check my own line, an extension of his, and immediately understand why. Tony from shipping and processing, again. It's the dozenth time this week. Luke's about to pick up the line when I hold up a palm to signal him, and mouth, *Let me.*

"Tony?" I pick up, my voice sweet as honey.

There's a pause on the other end. "Celia. I was looking for Luke."

"Of course. Unfortunately, he's unavailable right this moment. Can I help you instead?"

Another, longer pause. Tony hates dealing with me. I suspect it's because he doesn't like answering to women, which is why I enjoy making him. Finally, he lets out an audible sigh over the line. "We're going to be late with the Tuesday shipment—"

"Why is that, exactly?" I keep a smile on my face, because I swear you can hear that kind of thing over the phone.

Through the window of his office, Luke's expression is torn somewhere between annoyance and relief that I'm handling this. Like I always do. There's a reason I'm paid the big bucks.

I'm good at this. At handling every annoyance the world throws our way. Luke is the ideas guy, great at leading the company and developing new wild plans for where to take it. But I'm the one who excels at follow-through. I get things done.

Tony rambles through a million explanations, all of which I've heard before. They boil down to crappy excuses for why he hasn't been doing his job.

"So there's no way you'll have the shipment processed in the next five days?" I clarify. "In that case, why don't

I just call Morgan and her crew." The

night shift in the warehouse and

Tony's mortal enemy. "We can afford

to pay them overtime if it will make

the difference here."

Tony hesitates. Clears his throat.

I know he's weighing his options. Get

the overtime pay himself and actually

do his job? Or continue making bad

excuses and give up the overtime pay

—and the credit—to his arch-nemesis?

I smile at my reflection in my computer screen. I've got him.

"No, you know what, we can make it," Tony says. "If it's all right to add in a few overtime shifts for my guys..."

"Of course." My smile widens. "Thank you so much for all your hard work, Tony." I hang up and call through the open door. "You're welcome."

Luke winks. "You're an angel,

Celia."

An angel. My heart skips a beat. I file that away, into the mental file filled with every compliment Luke has paid me in the past year. Ever since I got promoted out of the general secretarial pool and into my position as head assistant for Luke Rossfield, President and CEO. Billionaire genius inventor.

Hottest man I've ever met.

The office is small, practically

start-up sized, which means, in about thirty minutes when everyone starts to file out for lunch, it's not long before I'm left solo at my desk. Luke has a 12:30 lunch meeting that will run overtime, I'm sure. It always does when he meets with this particular investor. The rest of our staff tend to take long lunches on Thursdays, and they'll be especially long today, on the first sunny Thursday of spring. This weekend is a long weekend too. Extra motivation for everybody to take a long lunch.

My hands move as if they have a will of their own. I open a website and follow my history trail through to one of the most frequently visited sites on my computer, as embarrassing as it is to admit. It's a "reality fanfiction" forum, mostly filled with people's fantasies about NFL players or rock stars or even particularly sexy bartenders they've run across in real life. Those are the rules. You can contribute any sexy story you want, but they have to be about a real person—fake name used to disguise them, of course.

It's the first and *only* place I've ever confessed my feelings for Luke.

It started out so innocently. Just a couple of fantasies late at night when I had trouble falling asleep, early on after my promotion. I swear it's because we'd spend such late hours together at the office; I wouldn't be able to hear anything but his voice by the time I got home, or picture anything but his sexy exasperated smirk, as we discussed one issue or another.

Then it progressed to imagining what I *wish* would happen in those office after-hours meetings. I'd picture him shutting the office door behind me and instead of starting to complain about regulatory guidelines, he'd pin me against the door and kiss me, telling me he just can't keep his hands off me for one second longer.

Eventually, I started to write out some of the fantasies. Just a couple of them. Just for myself.

Then I found this site, and posted one of them, only to suddenly gain an enormous following. Now I have readers begging for another installment.

I have other readers begging me

to just make a move already.

If this Liam—that's my

pseudonym for Luke online, to protect

his real identity—*is anywhere near as*

hot as you say, girl, you need to get on

that before somebody else does. That's

the most recent comment on the story

I posted a few days ago.

I do another quick check around

the office and scroll back up to the

top, to reread what I wrote.

"Cecily." Liam reaches up to tuck a

single strand of hair behind my ear. But

his hand lingers on my cheek, for just a

beat too long, his gaze fixed on me.

"How long has it been?" he asks, his

voice a low murmur.

Behind us, I'm all too aware of the

empty floor, our colleagues long since

checked out for the night. The lights are

out, everywhere but here in his office,

where he has a single lamp burning

beside his desk. It's not much

illumination. Just enough for me to

make out the searing heat in his eyes. "A year," I say.

"A year of working with you." His hand slides down my cheek to cup the back of my neck. He tugs me closer, and I can't help it. I step toward him, my hands sliding up to rest against his chest. I savor the warmth of his body, the feel of his muscles underneath my fingertips. "A year of torture."

My lips part in surprise. I start to step back, hurt, but his other hand *slides around my waist and holds me*

close. Pins me against him, until my

supple body melts into his muscular

one.

"Because I haven't been able to

touch you, Cecily. I haven't been able to

tell you how I really feel..."

My head tips back, my eyes fixed

on his. "Liam, we can't. There are rules

—"

"Fuck the rules." He kisses me, and

it's everything I've ever wanted. His

mouth is soft and sweet and tastes

faintly of smoke, just like the cologne he

wears. He spins me around, and my

back bumps up against the desk. Then

he's lifting me onto the edge of it, the

wood digging into my thighs, as his

hands slide down my waist to the

bottom of my skirt. It's office

appropriate attire, but the second he

gets his hands on it, it no longer feels

like it. He hikes the skirt up my thighs,

and slides a warm hand between my

legs, caressing the sensitive skin in a way that makes me shiver from the top of my head all the way to my toes.

"Cecily," he whispers again, against my mouth. "I want you so fucking badly I can hardly stand it. Every single day we're in this office together—"

"Celia?"

I jump so badly I nearly spill my coffee all over my desk. I slap the button to darken my desk monitor and leap to my feet all in one motion, heart in my throat. "Luke! I thought you left for your 12:30 already." I plaster on a huge, fake smile, and pray he doesn't read too much into my flushed cheeks. I wonder if he can hear my heart pounding. It's deafening to me. If he can't, it's a miracle.

"Sorry." He's grinning, amused. "I didn't mean to startle you."

"You didn't," I lie. God, I'm a terrible liar.

He glances away from me, and nods at the monitor. "I didn't mean to interrupt your, ah... *alone* time."

Alone time. Did he see my screen? Oh, god, did he guess what I was doing? "I just didn't hear you coming. Did you need something?" Deflect, deflect. Anything to keep him from asking too many questions about why I just panicked and turned off my computer screen.

"Actually, yes." He nods past me

toward his office. "It's a bit... sensitive, though. Could we talk in private?" He doesn't wait for my response, just strides past me into the office.

I cast another panicked glance around the floor, but there's nobody else here, no one who can spare me from this. My heart sinks. Luke never asks me to speak in private, much less about sensitive issues. He's normally an out in the open kind of boss. The only time he shuts his door is if he needs to tell someone they've done something wrong.

Which means this is it. He knows I've been writing dirty fantasies about him. He caught me reading them at work—what was I thinking? —and he's about to tell me he needs to move me to another department.

Heart in my throat, I step into his office. The second I shut the door behind me, Luke gestures to the chair across from him. Oh no. Worse and worse. We don't normally stand on ceremony, not between us. If he wants me to sit, it must be bad news.

I perch on the edge of the chair, too nervous to sit back or relax. "What is it?" I ask, eager to get it over with. I've never liked waiting, especially for bad news. I'd rather just rip this band aid off straight away.

But Luke leans back in his chair and considers me for a long moment. Dragging it out. His gaze drifts past me to the windows and back again, like

he's double-checking that we're alone.

Finally, he sighs. "There's no easy way

to say this, Celia."

I clench my fists in my lap and

resist the urge to shut my eyes, to

brace for the blow.

"Will you be my wife?"

CHAPTER TWO

My jaw drops. I feel like the floor is tipping out from under me. Like I've just fallen headfirst out of reality and into a daydream.

But then Luke catches my expression and adds quickly, "Pretend to be, I mean. Only for the weekend."

I let out a breath I didn't realize I

was holding. I'm pretty sure my face is bright red, and hot enough to light a cigarette off of. "Um... *what*?"

He laughs softly. "It's stupid, I know. It's just, I have this weekend trip planned with my friend Paul and his fiancée, out at the DelMonte—"

"That new hotel with the five-star chef that everyone's been talking about?" I interrupt.

"Out on the shore, yes, that one." He smiles. "Anyway, my friend and I had a bet going, a few years ago,

about who would get married first. He

kept insisting it would be him, because

I'm married to my job."

I blink and bite back my

instinctive response, which is *Aren't*

you? I can't help but think about the

fact that, in one whole year of working

directly with Luke, day in and day out,

I have never seen any evidence of him

dating. And I handle just about

everything for him, all the way down to

scheduling his barber shop visits and

sending out his dry cleaning. If there

were girls in the picture, I'd have seen

evidence of it by now.

Unless he's hiding it from you.

Unless he knows you have feelings for

him, so he makes sure to hook up on the

down-low. Unless...

Okay, so there's a possibility he

has hookups. But nobody long-term,

not in all the time I've been here.

"So..." I narrow my eyes, trying to

follow Luke's train of thought. "You want me to pretend that we're married, so you'll win the bet."

Luke grins. "Now you're getting it. Since Paul's wedding is in just a couple of weeks, I don't have much time left to beat him to the punch."

I sigh and cross my arms, pretending to deliberate, or at the very least to be hesitant about this proposition. But deep down, I already know what I'll say. I can't remember a single time I've managed to say no to

this man. Especially not when he's

looking at me the way he is now, with

that huge, charming grin of his, his

gaze focused on me like I'm the only

person in the whole wide world he

sees.

"It's just for two days, Celia, I

promise. We can have whatever we

want at the restaurant every day—I

hear the menu is seasonally themed

and rotates based on whatever the

chef selects from the neighboring farms. Plus, the DelMonte has its own vineyard..."

"Okay, okay." I burst out laughing. "It's like you know my weaknesses are food and wine, or something."

"Well, we have spent a decent amount of time together." His eyes sparkle with amusement.

I lean forward and have to catch my breath when he mirrors me. "Is that why you're asking me to do this?"

I arch one eyebrow. "Because we can fake a relationship easily?"

Some expression I can't quite read flickers across his face. But it's only for a split second, there and gone. Then he grins. "But of course. Who better? You know more about me than anyone on the planet, Celia." He sits back in his chair, palms flat on the desk. "But it's a big favor. I won't pressure you. If you don't want to—"

"I accept," I blurt out, before he can rescind the offer. Or worse, before he can ask someone else to do it. The last thing I'd want is to spend the weekend here in the city, picturing him off gallivanting around this gorgeous new hotel with a hot young bimbo on his arm, taking *her* out to fancy meals and then back to their big shared hotel room, where he'd probably have her for dessert.

I pinch the underside of my arm

to keep myself from getting too

distracted by my imaginary jealousy.

Or by the fantasy it turns into, when I

picture myself there with him instead.

"Wonderful." Luke hesitates for a

second, like he thought this would be

a longer conversation. "I'll drive. Can I

pick you up Saturday morning, first

thing?"

"I'll add it to both of our

calendars today." I smile in response.

"Be sure to pack your bathing

suit. And I'd say dress well, but of

course, your style is always

impeccable. Actually..." He glances at

me sideways.

I laugh. "Yes, I can put together a

wardrobe for you as well, if you'd like.

Your favorite suit should be back from

the cleaners by then."

"Perfect." Luke stands up, still

smiling, and crosses around the desk

to touch my shoulder. I freeze,

wanting nothing more than to linger

there, his hand on my bare shoulder,

his fingertips strong and smooth

against my skin. "Thank you, Celia. I

promise you won't regret this." He

winks. "Even if you're stuck with me, a

weekend at a luxury beachfront hotel

should be worthwhile, I hope."

His hand lingers so long that I

finally work up the nerve to reach my

own hand toward his, about to touch

my fingers to his. But at that moment,

he releases my shoulder, and my

hand touches my own skin instead. I let out a faint sigh, hoping he doesn't notice. But he's already crossing the office behind me to open the door.

I swallow hard and manage to recover some of my vocal abilities. "I'm sure it will be lots of fun." I force myself to stand and smooth down my skirt, before I turn to face him. I wonder if I imagine the way his eyes jump to mine, as if he were just looking somewhere else a second ago.

Probably. "Even if I have to spend it with my boss," I add with a wink, before I cross out of the office ahead of him and point to the clock nearby. "You'd better hurry if you want to make your 12:30 at this point," I call back to him.

There's a long silence. Long enough to make me turn back around to watch Luke as he walks to the elevator, his gaze never leaving mine. "Thanks, Celia," he repeats. A refrain I'll never get tired of hearing. "As always, I'd be lost without you." The elevator arrives, but he barely seems to notice. His eyes stay fixed on me, and he opens his mouth again, about to say something.

I lose my nerve and look back at my computer screen, only risking turning it back on now that he's on the other side of the office, too far away to accidentally glimpse what's currently pulled up on it. When I look back up, Luke's already gone.

CHAPTER THREE

At 8am sharp on Saturday morning, I
hear a car horn tapped lightly outside
my window. I stick a hand out and
wave to signal that I've heard and I'm
on my way. Then I grab my weekend
bag and sling it over one shoulder,
casting one last glance around my
apartment and praying that I've

remembered everything.

The bag weighs about a thousand pounds. I wasn't sure what exactly to bring—careful research of the DelMonte's website told me it's a lot fancier than the type of restaurants or resorts I usually visit with friends. Those are more of the budget-resort-in-the-Caribbean variety, and even then, we normally only go if there's some kind of package discount deal.

I've never been somewhere like

DelMonte. And Luke's compliments about my style aside, I'm not sure the outfits I own are fancy enough for this place, no matter how well-coordinated they might be. Rich people can spot knockoff designer clothes from a mile away, I'm told.

I don't know many ultra-rich people aside from Luke, and he's not that kind of person. He barely even notices if his own socks match, let alone if someone else's outfit is particularly posh or not.

Finally, I decide I've packed as well as I possibly can, and I close the door shut behind me and head downstairs. I threw on a cute sundress and hope it's the right thing to wear to something like this.

On the curb, I pause. Luke brought the Tesla. That means he's really showing off today. I suppress a smile and wonder who exactly this friend of his is. I've never heard Luke mention a Paul, but if his other close

friends and acquaintances are

anything to judge by, he's probably

from one of the other big competing

tech firms.

Luke has a one-track mind, and

that track is work. If you ask me, Paul

made a smart bet with him years ago,

gambling that Luke would never

commit to anything other than his

office.

The thought makes my heart

sink a little, at least until I hear the driver's side door open. Then my heart stops altogether.

Luke looks resplendent in his favorite suit, the one I had pressed and steamed for him the other day. He comes around to my side of the car to take my bag, before opening the passenger door for me with a wink.

"Don't you think you're exaggerating a bit?" I ask, even though I have to suppress a grin to do it.

"Husbands don't really open doors or carry their bags for them anymore."

"Yours does," he replies, in a low, confidential voice that makes my chest constrict. As I step past him to slide into the car, his hand brushes my arm, just for a second and lightly enough that it could be a casual mistake. But it's a mistake that makes my belly tighten and my thighs clamp together.

What am I doing? For the first

time, the full weight of what I've agreed to do this weekend hits home. Do I really think I'm going to be able to conceal my feelings for Luke all weekend? Especially in such close quarters, when we're *pretending to be married*. My heart races as I watch Luke in the rearview, loading my bag into the trunk and then coming around to his side and settling in behind the wheel.

"I could have driven myself, you

know," I babble, before my face flushes. "I mean, thank you, but—"

"Husbands drive their wives." He hesitates before he puts the car in gear and turns to face me. "Celia, I just wanted to say, before we go... I really need to go all in on this charade. Is that all right with you?" He smiles, a hint of mischief sparkling in his eyes. "If you want to back out now, I won't blame you. Like I said, I know it's a lot to ask."

I square my shoulders, ignoring the rabbiting of my heart. No matter how worried I might be about my real feelings showing this weekend, there's no way I'm backing out now. The last thing I'd do would be to leave Luke in a lurch. Especially one like this.

His hand is resting on the gear shift. Tentatively, I reach out to touch it. He flips it over and catches my hand in his, threading our fingers together. It's a more intimate touch than we've ever shared, and I catch my breath at

the sensation of his strong fingers

between mine. It makes me imagine

what they'd feel like on other parts of

my body. Sliding up my arms and then

down my curves, following them

around my waist to cup my ass and lift

me up off this car seat...

"I told you I'd help, Luke," I say,

and I pray my voice doesn't sound as

funny or strained to him as it does to

my own ears. "I'm not going to back

out on you now." I squeeze his hand

once, and release him, my fingertips

tingling where we just touched.

"Besides, you promised me some five-

star meals. I'm not about to miss out

on those."

He laughs and puts the car in

gear. "Good to know what kind of

things can tempt you, Celia. Food,

wine... anything else on your list of

irresistible temptations?"

I bite my tongue over the urge to

reply, *You*. "You've got the main ones down," I say instead, and roll down my window to enjoy the spring breeze as we head out of the city toward the shore.

The drive is beautiful, all the more so because of all the glances I'm able to steal of Luke while he drives. With his focus on the road, I can enjoy drinking him in more than I'd usually dare. He's smiling, relaxed, and chatty as we go. He tells me all about Paul—

an old friend from college who's a partner at a huge law firm in New York now. He tells me about the beach and the hotel. About how much he needs a break.

"But you're the one who really deserves it," he adds, just before he bends forward to point through the windshield. "How's she look?"

My eyes widen as I take in the veritable castle we're driving up to. It's set on a cliff high above the Pacific, the waves crashing onto white sand beaches far below. Up here, the hotel sprawls into four wings, looking more like a palace that belongs in Europe than here in SoCal. But I'm not complaining.

We pull up to the main drive, and a valet opens the door for me, then offers a hand to help me out of the car. Before I can lift a finger, another hotel valet has opened the trunk to remove our bags.

"We'll bring these to your room,

Mr. Rossfield," he says, already

hustling inside. I move to follow, but

Luke stops me with one hand on my

elbow.

"I almost forgot." He draws a

small box out of his pocket, and my

heart does a painful skip in my chest.

Is that...?

"We have to make this

convincing, don't we?" With a grin, he

pops the lid and offers up one of the

most beautiful diamonds I've ever seen.

I inhale sharply, mostly to try and keep my composure. It's a princess cut, with a white gold band. It's everything I ever imagined, and in my wildest dreams, my own wedding ring might look like it one day. *At least I can say I had it for a few days,* I think, as Luke slides it onto my finger, his eyes on my face to gauge my reaction.

I'm grinning like an idiot. I try to

tamp it down, but there's no disguising

this. "It's beautiful," I whisper.

He leans in to kiss my cheek, his

lips lingering against my skin for the

barest breath of a second. "Only the

best for my wife." Then he presses a

hand lightly against the small of my

back to guide me forward, into the

hotel.

It takes me a second to

remember how to walk. If this

weekend didn't feel like a dream

already, now it *definitely* does. I

suppress a shiver and cross the hotel

lobby, trying my best not to look at the

ring on my finger. Trying not to let

myself fall for the lie. *It's just a bet. One*

weekend.

But damn, what a weekend it's

going to be.

The bellhops see us straight into

the elevator, but inside, they just push

the floor for us and step back out

again, leaving us alone as the door

slides shut. Luke turns to grin at me.

"We should practice, you know. Before we have to perform for an audience."

I arch an eyebrow. "Practice what, exactly?"

His smile remains fixed in place, but there's something new in his eyes now, a spark that wasn't there before. A heat. "Kissing," he says, and before I can react, he's reaching up to cup my cheek and tilting my face toward his.

I've imagined this moment a

hundred times before. But I never

imagined it quite like this—how warm

his palm would feel cupping my cheek,

or how I would catch his scent

beforehand for a second, a hint of

smoke and spice. My eyes drop to his

lips, and I have just enough time to let

them flutter closed before his lips find

mine.

The kiss is soft at first. Hesitant.

He kisses me like I'm delicate,

breakable. But then I reach up to

twine my arms around his neck and

kiss him back. The moment I do, his

free hand slides around my waist,

pulling me against him, and his lips

part as he deepens the kiss, his

tongue slipping past mine to claim me,

completely.

I can't help it. He tastes even

better than I imagined, feels so much

more real than I ever pictured. All my

fantasies, all my fanfiction stories,

they pale in comparison to the reality

of his warm, muscular body pressed

against mine. *This is Luke,* I remind

myself. *This is really happening.* It feels

like I just wandered into a dream.

His hand slides down my waist

to my hip, his fingers digging into me

through the fabric of my thin

sundress. I arch one leg around his,

and I can feel the hard press of his

cock against my belly, thick and

throbbing through his pants. I moan

into his mouth, unable to help it,

because *fuck he feels so good.*

The moment I do that, though, he pulls back, chuckling softly, those searing blue eyes of his fixed on me as he laughs. "Maybe you don't need any practice after all, Celia." He reaches up to tuck a strand of hair behind my ear, one that escaped as we kissed. His hand lingers against my cheek. "You've got the horny newlywed act down perfect."

My cheeks flush bright red, and

his grin deepens, like he knows exactly

how wild he's driving me. But before I

can respond, the elevator reaches our

floor, and he takes my hand to lead

me out of it, down the hallway, toward

the suite that we're sharing.

My heart races in my chest, my

whole body still tingling. It feels like

my lips are on fire from his kiss, my

hips still seared by his touch. I can't

help it. I risk a glance down at my

fingers, where the ring he gave me

sits, right where it would if this were all real. If he really were my husband.

I decide that, just for this weekend, it will be all right to let myself believe it. I know it will only make everything harder once this is over and we're back at the office once this fantasy inevitably ends. But... I can't shake the look in his eyes when he kissed me, either.

So I decide, just for the weekend, I'll throw caution to the wind.

CHAPTER FOUR

The first thing that catches my eye

when we cross into our room is the

welcome note the hotel staff left on

our bed. There's a bottle of

champagne chilling in a bucket of ice

on a stand beside the bed, and in

front of it, a short letter welcoming

"Mr. and Mrs. Rossfield." Just the sight

of those words, a casual listing of me with his last name, like it's normal, like we're greeted that way every day, sends a thrill through me. How many times have I written fanfiction where that happened? How many times have I daydreamed about how good Celia Rossfield sounds?

My whole body tingles. Especially when I glance up at the rest of the room, with its huge windows overlooking the grounds below, a balcony outside, and a jacuzzi-style hot tub in our enormous en suite bathroom. "Did you actually book the honeymoon suite?" I ask, grinning.

"Of course." Luke winks and steps closer to me, his gaze fixed on mine, that hungry expression in his eye again. "In a way, this weekend is like our honeymoon, isn't it?"

I force a laugh, because I hope it will disguise the fact that my heart is racing, my pulse pounding. "Our pretend one, of course." But I can't

keep my voice even, or my eyes off his

lips. All I can think about is how he

tasted when he kissed me in the

elevator. How he'd taste if he kissed

me again, right here, right now.

When I glance back up at his

eyes, forcing myself to stop staring at

his mouth, I notice his gaze doing the

same thing. Jumping back to my face

as if he wasn't just checking out my

lips, my body. My cheeks flush with

heat, but he's already turning away to survey the room.

I do the same, walking across to the balcony and sliding open the doors. It's a beautiful day outside, the weather just right, warm not too hot. I step out onto the balcony and breathe in the fresh air, the scent of flowers growing along one side of the hotel. From up here, I can see the pool, huge and luxurious, with full beds around it rather than lounge chairs, and massage stations set up nearby, along

with a swim-up bar. Farther away, I

spot what look like outdoor hot tubs,

and little wooden shacks beside them

that must be steam rooms or saunas.

Beyond those, a series of flower

gardens.

In the other direction is a scenic

clifftop overlooking white sand

beaches and the ocean far below,

crashing against the rocks. The view is

beautiful, breathtaking. It will be even

more so at sunset tonight, I'm sure.

The thought of coming back to this

room with Luke tonight has my pulse

racing and my mind leaping toward

dirty thoughts.

I didn't think, when I agreed to

this, that anything would happen

between us necessarily. It seemed like

too much to hope for. But after that

kiss in the elevator, I can't help

wondering if he has more in mind

than just playacting.

When I turn back into the room to call Luke over, I catch him staring at me, that unreadable look in his eyes once more. "You look beautiful," he says, his voice so low I'm not sure I heard him right. He walks toward me, and I step back into the room to meet him, my heart racing.

"Thank you." My cheeks are still flushed from earlier, and the heat flows back into them now, especially when I watch the way his gaze drips over my body, like he's drinking me in.

"You look... great, too." My voice

faltered before I could say what I was

really thinking. *You look hot enough to*

set me on fire.

Luke winks in response. "There is

one catch, though, Celia." He lifts a

hand to trail along the wall closest to

our bed. Luke taps lightly. "My friend

Paul booked a room just on the other

side, right next to us."

"Oh." My eyes dance from the

wall to Luke and back again. "What does that mean?"

He grins and walks toward me, to where I'm standing in between the open windows of the balcony. "I'm very competitive, you know."

I have to suppress a real smirk at that. "Oh really? I didn't notice—how many times did you make the whole office play that card game Carl taught us, until you finally got good enough to win every single round?"

He smirks back. "Pretty sure I started winning by the end of the first night."

I narrow my eyes. "Still. What about your competitiveness?"

He tilts a head back toward the wall, nodding at it casually. "Well. I'm competitive about my marriage, too."

"Obviously, or you wouldn't have brought me all the way out here just to win a bet."

He loops an arm around my

waist and pulls me against him,

startling me. I suck in a breath, my

eyes locked on his, which are suddenly

just inches from my own. His face is so

close I can feel his breath caress my

cheek. My lips burn all over again,

longing for his once more. "I don't just

want to win this bet, Celia, I want to

dominate it." The way he says

dominate makes me clench my thighs

together, suddenly all too aware of the

heat between them, and how wet I'm

starting to get just at the thought of that. "I've already got a smoking hot wife. But I'll need Paul to hear just how hot our marriage is, too."

"H-hear... what, exactly?" I manage, proud of myself for only stammering a little bit. My heart trips in my throat.

"How hot our sex life is, of course." His hand slides down my curves, tracing the line of my waist to my hips. My heart beats faster, especially when he pulls me against

him again. This time there's no

mistaking the hard press of his cock

against my belly, still as hard as he

was before. It sends a thrill through

me, and makes my thighs clench

harder, my pussy already dripping at

the thought. Just knowing that I have

this effect on him, that I make him this

hard, makes me feel powerful,

seductive. Sexy as hell. "I'm going to

have to make you moan tonight,

Celia." He trails a single finger up the edge of my jaw, tilting my face toward his. Our lips are barely a breath apart now. I can hardly think; he makes my head swim so much. "I want our neighbors to hear you screaming my name with pleasure. So everyone who hears knows you're my sex-kitten of a wife." His fingertip reaches my neck, and he slides his hand around the nape of my neck, cupping me tightly. "So they know you worship your husband's cock."

I catch my breath, my eyes on his mouth. I couldn't look away now if I tried. "Well... if that's what we're going for..." I summon my nerve and meet his eyes, my own gaze probably hot enough to start a fire right about now. I want him so fucking badly. I have for months. For a whole goddamn *year*.

"Maybe we'd better start practicing again," I say, my throat almost closing over the words, over how bold that feels.

But to my relief, Luke doesn't balk at the thought, or back down. Instead, his smile just widens, sharpening around the edges. "You read my mind, Celia."

He kisses me again, and this time it's not tentative or hesitant. His lips sear into mine, and he walks me back one step, two, until I back up against the window next to the balcony doors. He flattens me against it, just before he pulls his mouth off mine. I gasp in protest, but he doesn't go far. He just tilts my head back, his lips tracing a trail down the front of my throat, his tongue darting into the indentation of my clavicle like he's tasting me. A full-body shiver goes through me, starting at the top of my head and working all the way down to my toes.

"God, Celia," he breathes against my skin, his breath even hotter than his tongue. I moan a little, parting my legs at a touch from his palm. He slides one hand between my legs, all the way up to cup my pussy through the fabric of my sundress, his fingers curling against me so strongly that even with panties on, I can feel their heat, and I can feel how wet I've become too.

"Are you as hungry for me as I am for you, Celia?" he whispers.

My clit feels swollen and heavy

with want. All I want is for him to keep

touching me, up until he spreads my

legs and fucks me. But his hand slides

away, back up my waist until he

reaches my breasts. One hand cups

my breast tightly, massaging, as his

thumb runs over my nipple. Even

underneath my bra, I can feel myself

starting to harden. "Fuck yes," I

breathe.

"Tell me," he says, before he

goes back to kissing me again, licking

and nipping and sucking at the spot

where my neck meets my shoulder.

He's biting hard enough that it will

leave a mark, I know, but I don't care.

At this point, all I can think is how

badly I want his mark on me, like a

claim on my skin.

"I want..." I almost lose my train

of thought, as he nips at me again. I

catch my breath. "I want to feel your

cock inside me. I want you, Luke, I

want you to fuck me."

He pulls back, a single eyebrow arched. "I want to fuck *my wife*. Who do you want to fuck?"

I realize what he wants, and it makes my heart beat faster, my pulse pounding in my throat. I lock eyes with him, unable to look away. "My husband," I say. "I want my husband to fuck me, right here, right now."

His grin widens when I answer correctly. "Good girl." He reaches down to catch my dress in one hand,

and draws it up over my head, slowly

enough to make me shiver as the

breeze through the open balcony hits

my bare skin. He pulls it off and drops

it in a heap beside us, before he

presses my back against the glass

window once more. It's cool against

my back, almost as cool as his hands

are searing hot against my front. He

unclasps my bra and lets it fall next,

before leaning down to suck my nipple

into his mouth. My breath catches in

my throat and I arch against him,

pressing closer as his tongue swirls

around my hardening nipple.

"Fuck." I slide my hands up to

bury them in his hair, my nails running

over his scalp. He shivers, so I do it

again, scratching him as he tongues

my nipple, one after the next, his

hands wandering down to my panties

at the same time.

It takes me a moment to recover

my senses, but when I do, my hands

already know what I want. I reach for his shirt and draw it up and over his head, before tossing it on the floor beside us. *Fuck.* I always suspected he was built. After sending out enough of his clothes for tailoring, I know his measurements by heart. But knowing his numbers and seeing his body with my own eyes are two very different things.

Never mind touching him...

"God you're so fucking hot," I

murmur as I run my hands over his sculpted pecs, his washboard abs. He catches my eye, his own narrowed, and I realize my error. "Husband," I add, putting a subtle emphasis on the word that makes him grin.

"Like I said earlier." He glances down, just as he hooks one thumb under the side of my panties. I wore simple white lace ones today, just in case. He tugs them down and off in one movement, and they puddle around my feet at once. I shiver,

standing before him completely

naked. "Only the best for my sexy as

hell wife." He leans back in to kiss me

again, and I melt into his lips, even as I

reach down to grasp the clasp of his

pants and carefully undo the button.

He stops me with one hand and

steps back for a second, gaze roaming

across me.

"Wait," he says. "I want to look at

my wife for a moment."

I shiver, feeling his gaze almost like a physical touch on my skin, it's so hot. He doesn't bother to disguise the naked lust and hunger in his eyes as he drinks me in. It hits me all over again how surreal this is. That it's Luke, that it's finally happening. The moment I've wanted ever since I first stepped into his office to interview for my position with him, and knew I was completely fucked.

This is the first time I'll *actually*

get fucked. Finally. Months of tension

feel built up in me. A whole year's

worth. Deep down, somewhere in the

back of my mind, I know I ought to be

worried about this. About sleeping

with my *boss*, for God's sake. But I

can't bring myself to care. Not when

it's Luke.

Not when he smiles with

pleasure and evident approval, and

reaches down to undo his pants,

pushing them down and letting me

see the huge bulge in his boxers,

springing free at last. "God you are

perfect," he tells me. He steps close

again, and I push his boxers down,

feeling like I'm unwrapping a present

for the first time.

His cock is fucking magnificent.

Huge and thick, veined a little along

the shaft, with a thick, spongy tip and

a base so wide I need both hands to

wrap my fingers around him. Which I

do, stepping close so I can feel the

velvety smooth skin of his shaft against my belly even as I start to stroke him.

His eyes fall half-closed for a moment, and a low groan sounds from the back of his throat, before he catches himself. "Is this what you're hungry for, kitten?" he murmurs, low and throaty in a way I've never heard him sound before. His voice, pitched at that level, makes my toes curl. "You want your husband's cock inside you?"

"Fuck yes," I breathe. At the same time, I tighten my grip around his shaft and start to stroke him, slowly back and forth, savoring the velvet slide of his skin between my fingers, and the hard steel of his shaft beneath. I lean back against the window, and gasp when Luke presses one hand flat against my belly, only to slide it down, over my stomach, to press against the mound above my pussy.

"Let's see how wet my wife is for her husband." Luke slides his hand between my thighs, and with deft fingers, he parts my pussy lips.

They make a slick sound, and he smiles, one fingertip sliding between my lips to stroke along my slit. I gasp, feeling his thick finger press between my lips, especially when he starts to slide the tip of his finger back and forth, collecting moisture.

"You are a hungry girl." Luke

locks eyes with me and brings his fingertip up to his own mouth. He slips it into his mouth and licks my juices from his fingertip, in a move that makes me shiver with lust. His eyes grow hotter, dark with want, as he arches his body against mine. His cock presses against my belly, and I can feel a drop of precum gathered there smear across my bare skin.

"Spread your legs for me, wife."

I spread my legs wide and let a

moan escape as Luke starts to stroke my slit, back and forth. His finger toys around the edge of my pussy, before, with one last grin at me, he presses his finger into me. I gasp, my eyes widening, as he presses his finger deeper. He feels so fucking good. So thick inside me. "Oh, right there," I gasp, when his fingertip glides across my sensitive G-spot.

His smile widens. "So nice and wet for me. Wet, and tight, and..." He strokes that spot again, and another little desperate moan escapes me.

"Hungry."

"Yes," I pant, hardly aware of my mouth moving. "Yes, I'm hungry for you. Hungry for my husband's cock." I reach out for him again, but he doesn't give me time to stroke him this time. He catches my hands in his, both wrists in his one free hand, and slowly lifts them up over my head, before his lips find mine again, searing hot.

His tongue invades my mouth, tasting me, claiming me. He pins me against the cool glass window, and I know that outside there must be people on the lawns, in the pool, on the beach. I wonder if they can see me up here, my naked ass pressed against this window. I realize I don't even care. All I want is for Luke to make me moan again.

But he draws his finger out of me, and my lips part as I gasp in protest.

"Do you want more, wife?" His

eyes lock onto mine, white hot.

"Yes. Fuck yes." I can't look away

from him.

"Are you sure?" He's smiling.

Taunting me.

"Please. Please fuck me." I don't

care that I'm begging. I want him. I'm

done waiting.

His smile widens. "Anything for

my wife." He reaches down to grasp

the base of his cock and guides

himself to my entrance. The tip of his

shaft presses between my lips, against

my entrance. He hesitates there, head

tilted, as if thinking about something.

"Do you want me to use a condom?"

he asks, watching me.

My heart skips. I'm on birth

control, and besides, in this fantasy,

we're married. "You're my husband," I

say. "I want to feel every inch of you."

"Good," he whispers. Then he

arches his hips, and I cry out as his cock drives into my pussy, stretching my walls around him. "Because I want to fuck my wife raw."

Fuck. He's even bigger than he felt in my hands. But oh, god, he feels good, slowly pushing deeper and deeper into me. He pulls my body against his, his muscles searing hot, and he reaches down to lift up my thigh.

I raise my leg, wrapping it

around his waist, and he drops my

hands to catch my other thigh too.

Then he lifts me up beneath him, and I

wrap both legs around his waist, until

he's holding me in midair, naked,

pinned with my shoulders against the

window.

The motion makes his cock drive

deeper into me, until he's buried fully

inside me, in one sharp motion that

makes my head fall back as I moan

with pleasure. "Fuck yes, husband,

right there."

"You like feeling that?" he

whispers into the crook of my neck.

He draws back a little, then thrusts

into me again, and I savor every inch

of him, the way his cock strains my

walls, makes me feel so fucking full.

"You like my cock inside you, kitten?

Who knew you were so damn dirty?"

He grins at me, and I grin back,

knowing my gaze is as hot and hungry

as his.

"You did, when you married me," I whisper, and he laughs, kissing me one more time, slow and hot, before he starts to fuck me in earnest.

He pulls out of me and drives back in with enough force to make me gasp every time. I wrap both arms around his shoulders for balance, my nails digging into his back as I cling to him. He moves faster, drives into me harder, arching upward so that his cock drags along my inner walls with every stroke, driving me wild. When he runs his tip along my G-spot, it's all I can do not to come on the spot. I find myself panting, begging him for more, and he just smiles the whole time, watching me, encouraging me.

"That's it, kitten, moan for me. Louder."

I remember what he told me about being competitive, and I'm surprised to realize how hot the idea makes me. The idea that other people will hear us, know exactly what we're doing in here. I *want* them to hear, I realize. I want them to know that I'm Luke's and he's mine, at least for this weekend, damn it.

"Fuck yes, right there, fuck," I cry out, my voice going louder, sharper.

"Are you going to come for me, kitten?" he asks, his voice louder too.

"Let me come for you, husband, please," I pant.

He finds a steady rhythm,

pounding into me again and again,

angled so his cock drags right along

my G-spot every time. It doesn't take

long for the pressure to build so high I

can hardly contain it, but then— "Not

until I tell you to, kitten," he orders,

and I can't help it. A faint cry of

frustration escapes me.

He chuckles. "Ask me nicely."

"Please." My voice is hot and low

near his ear. "Please, husband, I want

to come for you. Let me come on your

thick cock."

"Louder." He teases me again and again, taking me right up to the brink and making me beg at the top of my lungs before, with a smile that could break my heart, he relents. "Good girl, Celia. Come for me now."

It's all I can do not to burst. I scream with pleasure and relief all mixed together, as I finally let the orgasm sweep through me. My whole body shakes from the force of it, but

Luke just keeps going, fucking me

against the window, my bare ass

gripped tight in his hands. Before long,

I'm near the edge again. This time, he

holds me up with one hand and

reaches around with the other to slide

down and press his thumb against my

clit.

It's too much. I can't even ask

him for permission this time. I scream

as the orgasm sweeps through my

body, making sparks appear at the

edges of my vision. My toes curl, and my legs shake around his waist. My pussy convulses around his shaft. I'm barely able to cling to him, but I manage to, and then I lean in to kiss his neck, the side of his jaw. I hold on tight as he starts to fuck me harder, faster, clearly nearing the edge himself.

"Come for me, husband," I tell him, purposefully tightening the muscles in my pussy to clench hard around him. "Come for your wife."

"Celia." He calls out my name as he finishes, coming deep inside me. I can feel his hot juices spill into me, mixing with my own, and I cry out in pleasure, feeling how close he is to me, how tightly pressed together we are. When he finally steps back and releases my legs, just enough to pull his cock out of me, and let me stand back upright, I stagger a step, and he has to catch me, laughing, around the waist.

I can feel his juices spilling out of me, trickling down my inner thighs. God it's fucking hot. I tilt my head back to look at him, my eyes half-hooded with lust, and he leans in to claim my mouth in another slow, searing kiss.

"You are the perfect wife," he whispers when we break apart.

My heart skips a beat. I never knew how much I wanted to hear him say those words. But even now, still trembling from the feeling of his cock

inside me, I can't help but wonder how

long this can possibly last.

CHAPTER FIVE

I shower first, mostly because if I

don't, I'm not sure I'll be able to clear

my head enough from that orgasm to

function. I make the water hot and let

it wash all traces of sex away, even

though I swear my skin still smells like

him. I stick my face under the stream

and pray for it to wash away the dirty

thoughts that won't stop invading.

Thoughts of everything else I'd like him

to do to me next.

If that was only the practice run,

I can't imagine what Luke has in store

for later tonight...

Finally, when my skin has turned

red from the heat of the water, and I

smell like the hotel soap, a delicious

lavender scent, I step back out of the

stream and towel myself off. I already

picked out a different outfit, a skirt

and blouse that are a little fancier than the sundress I traveled in this morning. Besides, that's wrinkled on the floor by the window. And the panties I was wearing are soaked through, so I change those too. I hope I packed enough pairs of panties for the weekend, or I'm going to wind up going commando at some point.

My belly tightens at the thought of that, and at the thought of what Luke would do if he found me pantyless on some outing this weekend. I

drive dangerous thoughts of his lips

and fingers from my mind, and

hurriedly get dressed. Back out in our

room, I catch Luke still naked, smirking

as he leans against the window and

watches me exit the bathroom. Unless

I'm mistaken, he looks a little

disappointed I'm dressed already.

But, "My turn," is all he says, and

he crosses into the bathroom next. I'm

still drying off on the bed when there's

a knock at the door. I go to answer it

and freeze at the unfamiliar face on

the other side.

"Oh, uh…" It's a guy I've never

met, handsome enough in his own

way, though he can't hold a candle to

Luke.

The guy's face, on the other

hand, brightens with recognition. "You

must be Mrs. Rossfield, right?" My

heart skips a beat at the words.

Especially when he adds, "Luke's told

me so much about you." He sticks out a hand, and I stare at it for a beat, before I spot the woman beside him, also smiling. "I'm Paul," he adds, and it all clicks now.

"Celia," I say. "Nice to meet you. Luke's just getting ready."

"This is my fiancée, Meghan." Paul gestures over his shoulder, but Meghan's already sweeping past him into the room to hug me.

"So nice to meet you! I can't

believe you managed to tie down the infamous Luke Rossfield." Meghan swats my arm with a playful smile. "You must be every bit as amazing as Luke claims."

I laugh, wondering for the first time exactly what Luke told his friend about me. Did he make it all up? Or did he really tell them about me and just invent the marriage part? "I've heard great things about you both too," I say, mostly just to buy time. To be fair, Luke did say a lot of nice things about Paul, and that anyone who caught his friend's eye for the long-term must be special.

Luckily, I'm saved by the sound of the water shutting off, and moment later, Luke sticks his head out, a towel wrapped around his waist. "Paul! I thought that was you. Give me a minute."

"Your room is amazing." Meghan is pacing around it, wide-eyed with appreciative awe. I'm glad. It means

I'm not the only one who's not used to

staying in places like this one.

"Check out the view." I

demonstrate, to the sound of

appreciative gasps, while behind us,

Luke steps out of the bathroom, fully

dressed this time in a pair of jeans and

a loose button-down shirt, the top few

buttons undone. Still, he manages to

make me catch my breath, even

dressed casually like that. He looks like

he just walked out of a catalogue and into our room. I watch with appreciation as he grabs Paul in one of those tight, back-slapping hugs guys love.

Meghan catches me watching, and grins. "So the shine doesn't wear off once you're married? That's good to know." She glances down at her hand, where she's wearing a diamond almost as large as the one Luke bought me. I remember what Luke said, about Meghan and Paul's wedding coming up soon.

My throat tightens a little. I feel guilty, suddenly, about pretending to be some kind of wise married woman who could dispense advice. I don't know what I'm talking about—I'm just here playing pretend. But I force a smile anyway. "I find it hard to imagine a time when it could, to be honest," I say, because it's the most truthful thing I can.

Meghan sighs and smiles back happily. "I know what you mean." I catch her eying Paul in the same way, like she's drinking him in. It makes my smile turn genuine. "You know, I used to never think I'd settle down?" Meghan confides. She flashes me a sly grin. "I used to be kind of a wild child. But then I met Paul, and it was like... oh. Yeah. I could do this, with him."

"Trust me, *that* I understand." I fight back a smile as I turn to find the guys waving us over.

"We're going for drinks, come on." Luke waits until I reach his side, and then slings an arm around my shoulders, tugging me against his side in a casual gesture that sends my heart leaping into my throat. He acts like we've done this a million times before, and I love the feeling.

"So how did a guy like you wind up with such a stunner?" Paul jokes, flashing me a quick wink as he takes

Meghan's hand, with the kind of ease that makes me smile to see. They're a good match, the two of them. Easy with one another, relaxed. Plus, I can tell from the appreciative glances Paul keeps shooting his fiancée's way, they're both head over heels for one another. It's adorable.

Inspiring.

I elbow Luke, smirking. "Yeah, how *did* you win me over, exactly?"

He gazes down at me, eyes alight

with mischief, as we trail the others into the hallway and down toward the bank of elevators. "Well, it was in a similar resort to this one, actually, wasn't it, Celia? We'd been working together for a long time—"

Meghan fakes a scandalized gasp. "Ooh, so it was forbidden office love, then?"

"Something like that." Luke grins. "But then one weekend, we were finally able to get away from the pressures of work, and just be

ourselves with one another. I kissed

her in the elevator, and that was that.

Right, Celia?"

My cheeks flare bright red. *Does*

he mean now? But he can't. This is all

just part of the charade, isn't it? He

needed a convincing story for Paul, so

he used our real one, cleverly

disguised. I force myself to smile

easily, playing along. "Of course.

Though, you're leaving out the part

with the mind-blowing sex."

He said he's competitive with his friends, after all.

Paul and Meghan burst into laughter. Luke leans in to kiss my cheek. "Trust me, I would never forget that part." His gaze bores into mine for a moment, until the elevator doors ding open, breaking the tension. "I was just saving the best part of the story for last."

The four of us pile into the

elevator—the same one Luke and I

kissed in not so long ago—and

Meghan glances around us. "So, the

mind-blowing sex—did that happen in

the same elevator where you guys

made out, or...?"

"Should we be careful which

elevator we take in here?" Paul jokes,

and all of us laugh.

When we reach the ground floor,

we take a walk around the property

first. There's even more to the hotel

than we were able to see from our suite's windows. We pass tennis courts, a squash area, even an on-site vineyard, where you can go pick your own grapes, and learn more about wine processing from the hotel's vintners. There's also a full-service spa area that looks huge.

Meghan flashes me a grin when we pass that. "You and I are definitely coming back here at some point," she promises.

Finally, we reach the bar, set on the farthest side of the hotel from us. It butts right up against the cliff above the beachfront. There's a set of stairs near the bar that lead down to the beach, and the building itself sits close to the edge so that from the table we secure, we have a stunning view out over the sea. Down below on the beach, we spot people sunbathing, and a few intrepid surfers out battling waves in the deeper water.

Luke's the perfect gentleman, pulling out my chair for me and ordering on all of our behalf, since he's the most familiar with the wine list in this region. He's always been like this, even at work events, but I've never appreciated it as much as I do now, with the full force of his manners trained on me.

It makes me feel special in a way no guy ever has before. I can't remember the last time I felt like a real lady on a date, much less a pampered

one.

It doesn't hurt that, as we're

settling in after ordering, Luke scoots

my chair closer to his, and slides one

hand over to rest on my knee,

underneath the table. His palm is

warm against my skin, his fingers

curled lightly around my thigh, a

reminder of what we just did in our

hotel room not so long ago. A

reminder of how those fingers felt

inside me, as he pushed my back up

against the window.

I feel my breath hitch, and I

know I'm starting to get wet again just

remembering it. I try to think about

something, anything, else. At the same

time, though, I reach down to rest one

hand over Luke's, curling my fingers

around his as I lean in to listen to

Paul's story, about how he proposed

to Meghan. It's a cute story, in which

they were on vacation in the Swiss

Alps, and he was trying and failing to

teach her to ski, and he worried his

whole proposal idea was going to be

ruined because she just wanted to go

back inside and nap instead of taking

the lift up to where he'd planned the

thing.

But the whole time, Luke's hand

inches higher up my leg, and it's all I

can do to keep my gaze fixed on Paul

and Meghan, my smile normal, as we

both try to pretend nothing out of the

ordinary is happening here.

Finally, Luke's fingertips reach the edge of my panties, luckily hidden out of sight beneath the tablecloth. He shoots me a sly sideways smile and runs his thumb over the crease where my thigh meets my hip, just once, pressing hard enough to make a shiver run all the way from the top of my head to my toes. Then he draws his hand away, back to his own lap, and leaves me breathless and panting.

"What about you?" Paul is asking, oblivious to what just transpired, thank god. "How did you pop the question, Luke?"

"Oh, it wasn't anywhere near that elaborate." Luke launches into a story of his own, and I make all the right noises, nodding at the appropriate times, as he talks about taking me on a pretty drive through wine country and then just slipping the ring onto my finger at one point.

But all the while, I can't help

noticing neither guy has mentioned

this bet of theirs. You'd think that with

all the ragging they've done on one

another—and all of their digging

about how the other one met their

significant other—it would have come

up by now.

Then I glance at Meghan and

wonder if Paul told her about the bet.

Maybe not. Maybe he thought it

would be rude to mention the fact

that Luke gambled on Paul never finding a wife.

Doesn't matter. It seems like Luke and Paul are enjoying themselves, no matter who won their bet. Paul and Meghan seem genuinely happy. And it's nice to see Luke interacting with a friend who's not one of our coworkers or a potential client. His smile is just a little more carefree, his attitude even more open than he normally is. It makes me smile, too, watching him.

I can tell it's going to be a

weekend to remember.

CHAPTER SIX

Later that evening, just after we finish

an amazing three course meal, on a

different patio deck restaurant than

the one where we enjoyed our

cocktails, we stumble across a pool

party in full swing. There's a DJ playing,

and more than a few hotel attendees

decked out in their cutest, most

Instagram-worthy bikinis snapping poolside photos and dancing or posing on themed floaties in the pool.

"We have to go get changed and join this," Meghan yells in my ear, over the sound of the music. "Look, there's a jacuzzi free!" She springs forward before any of the rest of us can respond to claim a spot at one of the hot tubs next to the pool. I have to admit, with the night air beginning to cool down, and the jacuzzi bubbling and steaming, lit from below by lights

that change colors and pulse in tune

to the music, it does look pretty

appealing.

"What do you think, should we

let loose a little tonight?" Luke leans in

to murmur in my ear. The hum of his

voice tickles my insides and makes my

belly clench with desire. Especially

when he brings one warm, strong

hand to rest on my bare shoulder. I

shiver, and this time, it has nothing to

do with the faint chill in the air.

"Definitely," I manage to breathe,

leaning into him.

Nearby, someone chuckles. I

startle and glance over to find Paul

and Meghan grinning at each other,

then at us. "Meet you two lovebirds

back down here in a few, then?" Paul

asks.

My cheeks flush. But Luke

doesn't seem embarrassed by the fact

that his friends caught us snuggling. If

anything, to judge by the amusement dancing in his expression, he's enjoying it. Then I remember what he said, about being competitive. About wanting to show me off. A curl of heat unfurls between my legs. Something about the possessiveness, the showing off of how touchy we are, turns me on.

Even more so when Luke takes me by the hand and practically drags me into the elevator, with Meghan over his shoulder teasing us about not

getting *too* distracted up in our room

alone. I barely have time to wave at

her and promise we'll be right back

before the elevator doors shut and

Luke's kissing me against them,

hungry, his hands all over me.

I grin into his mouth and reach

up to twine my arms around his neck.

"I think your plan to make them

jealous is working," I whisper,

smirking.

"Good," he replies, his voice low and heated. He kisses me again, and then I forget all about his friends, the hotel, everything. All I can think about is Luke. His hands on me, his mouth on mine. When we break apart to hurry down the hall to our room, his eyes are fixed on me, hot as coals.

Inside our room, we barely make it through the door before he pins me against it. "We're definitely going to be late, aren't we?" I ask, laughing.

He grins against my neck before he kisses his way further down my body. "Not at all. We just need to get you changed. That shouldn't take long." As he speaks, he winds his hands around the hem of my shirt and yanks it up and over my head, dropping it beside us on the ground. His hands slide around to my bra now. He meets my eyes, his own sparkling with mischief. "Unless, of course, you think you're likely to get distracted by all of this. Are you, Celia?"

I swallow hard around a sudden

lump in my throat. "Not at all," I force

myself to say, keeping my voice even,

my hands steady. I reach for his shirt,

too. "As long as you won't." He doesn't

miss the challenge in my gaze, as I tug

his shirt off and let it drop beside us.

He bends back down to run his

tongue down the groove in the center

of my chest. I gasp and let my head

fall back, even as I run my hands along

his abs, tracing every inch of them,

while his tongue does the same to me.

God, it feels good when he does that.

It's like he's savoring every taste he

can get of me. His tongue circles my

nipple, lapping at it in slow, hard

strokes that make it stiffen.

At the same time, I tug on his

jeans, eager.

He pauses to smirk up at me.

"What was that you were saying,

about not getting distracted?" He

arches a single, perfect eyebrow. I resist the urge to run my thumb across it.

Instead I just smile as innocently as I can muster, pinned against a door half naked in front of him. "I'm just helping you along. Making this go faster." I wink, and then manage to get his belt buckle undone.

In response, his tongue dips lower. Past my breasts. I lose my grip on his jeans when he kneels in front of me, and I gasp a little, as his tongue

plunges into my navel, swirling around

it, flicking at the edges of it, in a way

that makes my belly tighten and my

thighs clench. My clit feels thick

already, swollen with want. I'm sure

I'm dripping wet, though I can't tell for

certain until Luke lifts my skirt with

nimble fingers.

"No fair," I whisper, my breath

coming harder and faster now. "You

stole my idea."

"I did warn you." His gaze flashes to mine, not a hint of regret in it. "I like winning."

I laugh, which quickly turns to a gasp as he pulls my skirt down and off my hips. My underwear slide after them and land on the floor.

When he glances back up at me, he's smirking, enjoying himself. "Spread your legs, Celia." There's a subtle note of command in his tone, one that makes me shiver with pleasure.

I obey him and spread my legs.
He doesn't waste any time. He plunges
between them, and I gasp aloud as his
tongue rasps along the edges of my
lips, tracing me. He runs his tongue up
and over my clit, just a quick barely-
there flick that nevertheless sends a
shockwave of pleasure through my
body, I'm already so eager for him.

"Fuck, Luke." I hiss through my
teeth, reaching down to bury my

hands in his hair in order to steady

myself.

"You taste so damn good, Celia.

Have I told you that yet?" His breath

feels even hotter against the parts of

my body he just licked, namely the

sweet, hot place between my thighs.

His tongue delves in again, and this

time, he presses it between my lips,

running along my slit, in a lapping,

come-hither motion like he's trying to

lick every drop of my juices from me.

I moan a little at the waves of

pleasure that sends through me. My

eyelids flutter closed, unable to stay

open, as he starts to lick me faster, in

slow, steady strokes that nevertheless

stoke the fire building deep in my

belly. My toes curl, and I arch up onto

them, my hands now fisted in his hair,

trying desperately to maintain some

semblance of control.

But it's not long before I'm

gasping and moaning his name under

my breath, the pleasure in me building

quickly toward a peak. He knows

exactly what he's doing, damn him.

I've never been with a guy who takes

this much time on me, making sure

my pleasure comes first.

"Right there, Luke, fuck, right

there," I'm gasping, when suddenly, he

pulls away, sitting back on his heels to

grin up at me. I let out a sudden

breath, still shivering. I was so damn

close... "Don't stop," I cry.

His smile widens. "I thought you weren't going to get distracted."

My breath is coming so fast it takes me a couple of seconds to even respond. "That... didn't count," I try, lamely.

He just chuckles and rises to his feet. "Don't worry." He leans in to kiss me, slow and soft. His tongue parts my lips, and I can taste myself on his lips, our scents mingled in a way that tastes heady, going straight to my brain. When we break apart, his eyes are fixed on me. He looks every bit as hungry, as filled with lust, as I am. "There will be plenty of time later tonight to make you scream. For now…" He reaches up to run his thumb across my lower lip. My eyes flutter half shut, and I part my lips to suck his finger into my mouth, twirling my tongue around him. He groans a little, biting his lower lip, gaze heated where it fixes on mine.

Two can play this game, Luke, I

think, smiling back at him.

He steps back, though I can see

by the huge bulge in his jeans that he's

not as unaffected by all this teasing as

he wants me to think. "For now, we

have a date to keep," he tells me, and

grabs his swimming trunks from the

wardrobe beside our bed. He catches

my eye with a smirk before he heads

into the bathroom to change. "Later?

Well. Later, I'd like to hear how

desperate you are to come.

Anticipation makes the release all that

much sweeter, in my opinion."

Easy for him to say. Still, I've

never been one to shrink from a

challenge. I lift my chin and keep my

gaze on him, a bemused smile curling

my lips. "Later it is, then," I say, even

though my pussy is practically

throbbing with the need for release.

Oh, I am going to get sweet revenge

on him for this move...

CHAPTER SEVEN

By the time we meet Paul and Meghan
back in the pool area, there's still a hot
tub free. My face is still flushed, my
breath a little uneven. But if our
friends notice, they don't say anything.
They just make room for us in the tub
with them. They look like they've been
amusing themselves plenty anyway—
Meghan is sitting in Paul's lap, and he

has his arms twined around her waist, casually. They're cute together.

I wonder if we'll look that cute together a couple years into being together. Then I shake myself, remembering. *This is just for the weekend.* It's just about the bet, nothing more.

But that's hard to remember when Luke slips into the hot tub next to me and pulls me onto his lap too, leaning in to kiss the nape of my neck sweetly, his tongue darting across my skin just for a second, as if to remind me of earlier, in the room. Of just how much pleasure—and frustration—he can cause with that tongue of his.

"You missed the DJ set," Meghan says. "But I think there's a new one coming on now."

"Thank god," Paul adds. "This one seems more chill." The music is low enough now that we can hear ourselves talk, which is nice. There's still a beat to it though, low and

steady, the kind that makes me want

to move.

Which gives me an idea.

I start to sway to the beat, back

and forth across Luke's lap. Under the

water, I can already feel the hard

press of his cock through the thin

fabric of his swimming trunks. It only

gets stiffer as I casually rub my ass

back and forth across it, a casual smile

fixed on my face, like I'm just dancing

to the music.

Behind me, I can hear Luke suck in a sharp breath. *See how you like a taste of your own medicine, teaser,* I think. When I glance back at him over my shoulder, his eyes are dark and filled with desire, fixed on mine in a way that tells me he knows *exactly* what I'm thinking. And why I'm doing this.

It makes my smile widen.

Across the hot tub, Meghan

slides off Paul's lap to dance a little,

too. "Actually, I really like this one. Do

you want to check out the dance floor,

hun?" She flashes him a wide grin, and

if I'm not mistaken, her eyes do a little

sideways dart toward us, quickly,

before she nods across the pool floor.

There's a small dance floor near the

bar, where a handful of couples are

entwined, swaying to the music,

especially as the beat starts to get

faster, more insistent.

Paul catches my eye, but only for a split second, quick enough that I could've been imagining it. Still, I get the feeling they know Luke and I could use a minute of alone time. "Sure." He grins. "I could use a drink refill too. You guys want anything?"

"Oh, I'm good," I say. Or I was about to say, anyway. But Luke speaks over me.

"Couple of champagnes would be great, thanks."

"Sure thing." Paul flashes us both one last wink, and then climbs out of the hot tub, helping Meghan after him. I barely wait until they're gone before I spin on Luke's lap and start to dance again, slower this time, rolling my hips against him in a way he can't miss.

I can feel the tense and jerk, as his cock jumps between us, so rock hard that I know he must be dying for release.

"Is this revenge?" he asks,

grinning, before he brushes my hair

back from my shoulder and leans in to

nip at the soft skin there gently.

"Maybe," I admit, slowly twisting

my hips side to side. "Or maybe I

always give my husband sexy lap

dances when we're in a jacuzzi

together."

"Mm... I married well, then," he

murmurs, his voice a vibration against

my neck.

I reach up to drape my arms around his neck and really start to get into the dance. I dip and drag my crotch along his, biting back a gasp as I feel the hard press of his cock dig into my swollen clit for a second. Then I spin in the tub and back up against him, grinding my ass along his thick shaft, undulating my hips and shoulders at the same time, so every inch of my curves is on display.

He tries to hide it, when I turn

again to slide my knees up along

either side of him, my thighs wrapped

around his. But his breath is hitching,

and there's no hiding the heat of

desire in his eyes.

His hands trace my sides. "You

are so goddamn sexy, Celia," he

murmurs, low and hot, with feeling. It

sends a thrill through me, almost as

much as when he had his tongue

inside me. It's a heady thrill, knowing

how hot I make him. Knowing that I

have the same effect on him that he does on me.

I spin again, my back to him once more, and shiver as he tightens his grip on my hips. He's the one leading me now, my body swaying in tune to his direction, as he moves my hips against him. I feel him arch up against me, the shaft of his cock digging into the soft, hungry place between my legs.

He leans in to whisper, breath

hot against my ear. "I think we've both

waited long enough, don't you?"

My breath hitches. "But..." My

eyes dart around the pool. "Should we

go—"

"I'm not about to walk anywhere,

thanks to you." He's grinning, as he

slides a hand over my hip to hook his

thumb through my bikini bottoms.

"Relax, Celia." I glance down at the

bubbles in the tub. "Nobody will see

us." He's right. The bubbles hide

everything below the surface from view.

Still, I can't help feeling a thrill of fear—mingled with excitement—as he tugs my bottoms to the side. I can feel him adjusting himself beneath me. His bare cock slides out of his trunks, and he runs it along my ass, pressing the tip between my lower lips, just far enough to touch my entrance and make me suck in a sharp breath. I am so fucking wet. So ready for him.

Still, he hesitates. "Do you want to come for me, Celia?" he whispers into my hair.

"Fuck yes," I pant. I've been dying for release ever since our trip to the room. Ever since he tongued me right up to the edge and them left me hungry for him. Eager to come.

"Tell me how much you want it, wife."

I tilt my face over my shoulder so my gaze can meet his. The music, the dancers, the rest of the pool, all the hotel guests… it all fades into the background. Right here, right now, there's only the two of us, alone in the world. "Please make me come, husband," I whisper. "Please. I need to."

"You need this?" His tugs my hips down against him, just an inch or two. Just far enough for the head of his cock to slip between my pussy lips.

"Yes, husband, I need your cock.

I fucking need it." We're both

whispering, low and hot. The water

swirls around us, the bubbles adding

to the sensations, tickling my skin,

making me even more aware than

ever of his every touch. His one hand

slides around my front so his palm is

flattened across my mound. Then he

uses his hand to pull me down onto

his cock, agonizingly slowly.

I groan under my breath, my

eyes fluttering half shut, as I feel him

slowly begin to fill me. He keeps going,

so deep inside me that it feels like his

cock is buried in my belly, straining

against my walls. His one hand

tightens on my hip, his other still

pressed against my mound—his

fingers touch just a centimeter above

my clit, like a taunt, like he's reminding

me how easily he could make me lose

my mind.

Dimly, I'm still aware we're in

public, in a pool area where anyone

could see. Where dozens of people are walking past us, dancing, drinking, laughing, singing. It turns me on even more, knowing how easily we could be caught. Knowing how we're right out in the open doing this.

Finally, he's all the way inside me. "Keep dancing," he says, low and commanding.

I start to move again, wriggling against him, and he bounces me up and down in his lap, just far enough to drive his cock in and out of me, but

not hard enough to make the water

churn, to make it obvious what we're

doing.

It's a kind of sweet torture. He's

not thrusting hard and deep, but short

and shallow, quick thrusts that drive

the head of his cock right along my

front inner wall, making me grit my

teeth as his spongy tip glides over my

G-spot again and again. It doesn't take

long before I'm poised on the brink of

orgasm, but he tightens his grip on my hips with both hands now, his fingers digging into my skin hard enough that I'm sure it will leave marks tomorrow. That only makes it hotter, somehow, the tiny tinge of pain in among the pleasure.

"Wait for me," he orders, his voice a low murmur against my ear. "Don't come until I do."

I hold my breath and dig my nails into my palms, trying to contain myself. But it's hard. I've been teased

all day and tormented up in the room

just before we got here. My body is

aching, dying for a release. Still, I

clench myself tight, holding it in. I can

feel him shuddering beneath me as he

thrusts a little harder, a little faster.

The water churns slightly around us,

but I'm too far gone to notice, to care.

He's nearing his edge too.

"Come in me, husband," I

breathe, tilting my head back so my

lips brush his. "I want to feel you fill me with your cum."

He grits his teeth and groans, low enough that nobody else can hear it over the music. Then he whispers, "Come now," and I can't hold it back any longer.

The orgasm hits me hard, making my whole body shake as I gasp for air. At the same time, I can feel him release too, shooting his cum deep inside me, pinning my body tightly against his with both hands. I hold myself there, shuddering with the aftershocks of ecstasy, my eyes half-closed with pleasure.

We hear voices coming closer, and we both glance up to see Paul and Meghan returning. Luke tugs me back against him, voice hot against my ear as he whispers. "Don't let anyone know. And don't let a single drop of my cum slip out of you into the water," he breathes.

Then he releases me, and pulls

out of me, at the same time letting his

fingers release my bikini bottoms so

they snap back into place. I clench

every muscle in my body, forcing

myself to act normal, to flash a smile

at Paul and Meghan as I climb out of

the tub on shaking legs. "Bathroom

run," I explain with a jaunty wave,

before I start to hurry across the

grounds. My breath is still coming fast,

my cheeks flushed. It's a good thing

my bathing suit is already soaked, so nobody will notice the cum that starts to leak from my pussy, dribbling down my inner thigh as I cross the pool deck to the bathrooms.

When I finally make it into a stall, I practically collapse against the door, my whole body trembling. My pussy feels so sensitive that even just cleaning myself up makes sparks of pleasure jump through my veins. I wait until my breathing has steadied before I venture back out of the stall

and try to plaster on a normal

expression, to return to the pool area.

Fucking hell. I'd always imagined

sex with Luke would be hot, but I had

no idea it would be like... well... *this.* So

hot that I'll be ruined for fucking

anyone else after this weekend.

I push the thought to the back of

my mind. We still have a whole night,

and tomorrow together, too. I don't

need to think about how temporary it

is yet. I don't need to worry about

what happens when this ends.

For now, I promise myself I'll just

enjoy the ride.

CHAPTER EIGHT

We stay at the pool party until it winds

down. Luke toasts me with

champagne, but I barely drink even

half the glass. I don't need it. My head

is already swimming with enough

endorphins to make me dizzy,

especially after we finally climb out of

the hot tub at the end of the night to

make our way back to the rooms. We

bid Meghan and Paul farewell at our

doors, with them heading into the

room beside ours with one final wave.

The moment the door closes

behind us in our room, Luke turns

back to me, grinning. "That was very

impressive, earlier." He reaches up to

brush a strand of hair back from my

forehead. "I had no idea you were

such a naughty girl, wife."

"Well, you must have married

me for a reason," I reply, smiling back.

There's a flash in his eyes for a

moment, some kind of emotion I can't

read. It makes my cheeks flush,

suddenly worried I said the wrong

thing. "I mean, fake married, of

course."

"Of course," he replies, his

expression still dark, inscrutable. Then

he drops his hand from my shoulder,

only to take my hand instead. "Come

on. We'd better get you dirty again."

He tugs me toward the bathroom.

I grin, trailing after him. "Don't you mean clean?"

He flashes me a heated look over his shoulder. "Not at all."

Inside the bathroom, he strips me down. I pull his trunks off, too, and it's immediately obvious that he's already hard again. Damn. Man has stamina, I'll grant him that. He notices me notice, and smirks. "I must admit, you have quite the effect on me,

Celia." He steps closer and slips one hand between my legs to cup my bare pussy, still dripping wet from the pool, and probably from renewed lust, too. After all, we spent a whole elevator ride up here in proximity to one another. Apparently just his scent is enough to make me horny now.

"You do the same thing to me," I whisper.

His fingers tighten, one slipping between my pussy lips. "I can see that." He draws his hand back and holds it to my lips. Obedient, I suck his finger between my lips and trail my tongue along his length. I can taste my own juices, sweet mingled with a hint of salt from his fingertips. I keep my eyes locked on his as I do, and swirl my tongue along the base of his finger suggestively.

"You really are a sex-kitten, aren't you, love?" His smile widens, his eyes taking on that dark, hungry expression that makes me shiver with

anticipation. My stomach flips when

he says the word *love*. Even though I

know he doesn't mean it, even though

I know this is a temporary

arrangement, I can't help it. I've

thought that about him too often, for

too long, to miss the word now.

"You could say that," I reply,

trying to hide the quiver in my voice,

and not quite succeeding.

Then he draws his fingertip away

and turns on the shower, piping hot,

enough to raise steam from the water.

It begins to fog the mirrors as he tugs

me into the shower with him. "At least

this little kitty doesn't mind getting

wet." He smirks and runs his hands

over my body as the heated shower

water cascades over me.

I reach for him too, unable to

keep my hands off of him for long. I

trace my hands down across the

washboard plane of his abs until I

reach the V of muscles that lead my

fingers down to his cock. He's hard as

a rock already, even after our

rendezvous in the jacuzzi. I have a

feeling Luke could keep me going for a

very, very long time tonight. And I

have to admit, I am not at all opposed

to the idea.

I slide my hands around the base

of his shaft, marveling yet again at

how thick he is, how strong he feels.

There's a solid layer of steel beneath

the smooth velvet glide of his cock,

and I stroke my hands along it, tracing

the veins along the sides, the tight

seam underneath. He sucks in a

breath through gritted teeth, and I

smile up at him from beneath my

eyelashes.

"Do you remember what I told

you about tonight, wife?" he asks.

I glance down between us at the

reminder. Don't get me wrong, I love

how even when we're alone he still

calls me that. And I love even more seeing the huge rock of a ring he gave me still on my finger, even as I start to stroke my hands back and forth, up and down the length of his shaft in a slow, rocking motion. It does something to my insides, makes me hotter than hell just imagining what it would feel like to be Mrs. Rossfield for real. Not just for the weekend, but forever.

"Um..." I realize he's still waiting

for an answer. I think back over

everything he's said to me so far

today. But it's been a long day, and

there are a lot of things I don't want to

forget, all warring for attention in my

mind. Not least of which is his voice,

soft and steady, telling me to come for

him earlier tonight. I suppress a

shiver. Then I remember what he

must mean. "That you're competitive?"

I glance sideways, toward the wall that

separates our room from Paul and

Meghan's.

His smile widens. "That I'm going to have to make you scream my name, again... and again..." His hands slip down my slick sides, over the arch of my hips, and part the soft flesh of my thighs. He presses one hand between them, his fingertip parting my pussy lips to stroke me again, back and forth in a come-here motion that makes my hips rock toward him.

I tighten my grip on his cock,

both to keep up and for balance, as

the pleasure starts to stir inside me.

"So you want me to be loud for you,

husband, is that it?" I smile up at him,

sly.

   "Very." He leans in and claims my

mouth in his. I sink into his kiss, letting

him take control. He parts my lips with

his tongue, at the same moment that

he presses his forefinger inside my

pussy. I'm a little sore already from

earlier, but the soreness is quickly

overtaken by pleasure as he starts to stroke his finger, in and out of me, the tip pressed against my inner walls. He curls his finger forward, and I groan into his mouth. He chuckles softly, and breaks the kiss, leaning back just far enough to study me with heated eyes. "But first, wife, my cock is still nice and dirty from our encounter earlier." He lifts an eyebrow, suggestive, and my face flushes with understanding.

Then again with desire.

I sink to my knees in front of him in the shower. There's a nice cushioned bath mat, which makes it comfortable to kneel, and I reach for his cock. "I can't wait to taste you," I tell him, and he chuckles again, running his hands through my hair fondly.

"My wife is so cock-hungry. Aren't you, kitten?"

"Starving," I tell him, glancing up to meet his eyes as I lean in and trail my tongue along the underside of his

shaft, all the way from base to tip in

one long lick. I love the view from

here. Him gazing down at me with

hooded eyes, his hands stroking my

hair as he pulls me back toward his

cock again.

And the taste...

When I lean back in, I cup my

mouth around the tip of his cock,

swirling my tongue against him, licking

and tasting. He tastes fucking

incredible. Like salt and heat and smoke, the same way that he smells but more concentrated, heady in a way that goes straight to my head, even more than the hot water still cascading over us both.

He groans a little under his breath, and I love that. I love knowing what an effect I have on him.

"That's right, wife, suck my cock," he murmurs, and draws me closer toward him.

I part my lips, obedient, and let

his cock slide along my tongue. As he

inches deeper, I slide my hands

around the backs of his thighs and

then up to grip his ass. *Damn.* He has

a seriously tight ass. Sculpted and

perfect beneath my hands. I tighten

my grip on him and it helps to balance

and brace myself when he thrusts a

little deeper into my mouth, his cock

sliding to the back of my tongue.

My body tenses for a second, as

my gag reflex threatens to kick in, but

Luke just strokes my hair again with

one hand, the other still fisted in it.

"Relax, Celia. Trust me."

So I let go. I let him have control.

And this time, when he holds the back

of my head and pulls me onto his cock

again, there's no shudder, no reflexive

choke. The tip of his cock slides past

the back of my tongue, almost hitting

the back of my throat. Then he pulls

back, and I suck in air, just before he

thrusts back in again. This time, he

does touch the back of my throat, and

inches down it a little, his cock

completely filling my mouth, capturing

all my senses. I moan around him with

pleasure and curl my tongue up

against him as he pulls out to rock

back in again.

He sucks in a sharp breath, and

starts to move a little faster, rocking

against me. "God, I love that sexy, tight

little mouth of yours," he murmurs.

"Suck my cock, wife, suck it like you're starving for it."

I tighten my lips around him and keep my jaw loose and relaxed, my tongue curled up against him. At the same time, I keep one hand tight around his ass for support and bring the other around to play with his balls, cupping and tugging gently on them.

He groans again, and I know I'm doing something right. He starts to rock faster against me, and I let him lead, using my mouth for his pleasure.

I love the way it feels. Like total

surrender. I moan again, and I feel

another shiver go through him.

"Fuck, Celia, you are... fucking...

perfect," he manages, his breath

coming in fits now. But just before he's

about to reach his peak, he pulls back,

out of my mouth, and I cry out faintly

in protest. He just chuckles, watching

me, as he leans down to help me back

to my feet. "Oh trust me, wife, we are

nowhere near done yet."

The heat surges back into me,

especially when he grabs my body to

pin me against the wall of the shower.

He lifts one of my legs, then the other,

holding me against the shower wall,

the steam curling around us. I wrap

both legs around his thighs, and cry

out when he enters me fully, in one

hard thrust.

He fucks me like that, up against

the shower wall, until I scream his

name with pleasure, the orgasm

hitting me sooner than ever, what with

how much he's been turning me on all

damn day. But he's not finished. He

carries me out of the shower, and I

wind up bent over the sink, my voice

echoing in the tiled bathroom as he

fucks me from behind.

"Come for me, Celia," he

commands, and I can't help but obey,

screaming with pleasure as the

orgasm hits me. This time I can't form

words, sentences. I'm too lost in the pleasure as he thrusts deep into me.

When he finally comes with a guttural growl that makes my belly clench in pleasure, my legs are trembling so hard I can barely keep upright, and my pussy feels sore and spent. But he takes care of me, gently toweling me off and wrapping me in one of the hotel's soft robes, before he carries me to bed and tucks me under the covers. When he climbs in beside me, I curl into his side, and he wraps

both arms around me.

I fall asleep with my head on his

chest, lulled by the steady, comforting

drumbeat of his heart.

CHAPTER NINE

I wake to the scent of coffee. Coffee, and something else, something delicious... Waffles?

I crack one eyelid to see Luke, still dressed in the hotel bathrobe with nothing underneath, setting up what appear to be trays of room service. I laugh under my breath, disbelieving, and move to sit up and join him. But he catches my eye and shakes his head.

"Lie back," he commands, and I can't help but obey. It doesn't hurt that my limbs feel pleasantly sore, my pussy tight and used from last night. Everything throbs, but in a way that reminds me just how much pleasure we found in each other last night. How fantastic he made me feel.

I pull over some additional

pillows and adjust myself so I'm sitting up against the headboard. Then Luke brings me over a tray, with a waffle on one side piled high with fruit, and on the other, a cup of coffee and an orange juice. He settles it across my lap before leaning in to kiss me softly.

"I wanted to bring my wife breakfast in bed," he tells me, still with the ever-present playful tone in his voice.

But there's something in his eyes that tells me he's getting more than just sexual pleasure out of this. He's actually enjoying this, spoiling me. For whatever reason, I can't quite fathom.

Still, I'm not about to complain. I pick up the coffee, smiling at him over the brim, and then hesitate, glancing at it with a slight frown. "Oh. Is there milk in this?" I'm judging by the coffee's paler-than-black color.

But Luke just grins, anticipating my hesitation. "You don't do lactose, right? I got you almond milk instead."

I blink in surprise. Yes, I know Luke's coffee order off by heart. But I'm the office assistant, and I normally wind up doing the coffee runs for everyone. I didn't realize he remembered my order too. Or why I drink almond milk normally. I smile and nod. "Thank you."

"Of course." He winks. "Anything for my wife." He picks up a tray of his own, and settles himself onto the foot of the bed, across from me.

"I didn't know you'd remember my coffee order," I add, after a moment of hesitation.

He laughs. "Why not? You've got mine memorized."

"I know, but..." My cheeks flush. I shake my head, losing my nerve. "Never mind."

When I look up again, I find him watching me more intently, that strange expression back in his eyes. "You know, Celia, I remember a lot of things about you."

"Oh?" I arch one eyebrow, smiling. "Like what, for example?"

"Like that you have two younger siblings, who both live up in Seattle now. You grew up in the Bay Area before you moved down here. Your parents are retired and live in San Diego. Your mom used to work in the forest services, and your father was a chef."

My eyebrows rise higher than

ever.

But he isn't finished yet. He curls one leg under himself and starts to gesture with his fork like he's conducting a PowerPoint presentation about me, getting into it. "You used to have a cat named Buttons, but you developed allergies, so you gave him to your sister. You miss having pets but you want to wait to get a dog until you, and I quote, "have the little white picket fenced house to go with one," and you look so goddamn cute when you blush and smile like that," he adds, winking at me again.

I burst into laughter. Mostly to hide the stupidly happy smile that's burgeoning on my face. "Luke..."

He shifts closer to me on the bed. His blue eyes are so close I feel like I could trip into them at any second, fall into his gaze and forget the rest of the world. "I remember a lot about you, Celia. More than you think." His gaze drops to my lips, as he tilts a fraction of a foot closer. I mirror him, until our noses are almost touching. "You're the kind of woman who makes me want to pay attention."

"Oh?" I can feel his breath on my lips, and I'm sure he feels mine on his. I bend a little closer, so my lips brush against his as I speak. "Why is that, exactly? Just because I'm irresistible?"

"Exactly." He grins, and then he kisses me, and fireworks explode in my belly, curling outward toward my fingers and toes, until every nerve ending feels electric. When we break apart once more, he smiles at me, softer this time. "And, because I'm the best husband ever," he adds, and I laugh again as he leans back over to pick up his fork once more.

We eat for a few minutes, me watching him out of the corners of my eyes and pretending to look away whenever he catches me. He shifts topics, talking about the day ahead of us, the spa we should check out in the hotel and the sunset drinks he's planned for us later. All the while, I can't shake his voice from my mind. *You're the kind of woman who makes me want to pay attention.*

All this time we've been working together, all the time that I've been secretly crushing on him and writing fanfics about an imaginary dream I never thought could happen in real life... Has he been doing the same? Has he been thinking about me like that too?

Or is this all just an act? All just a play for the weekend, to win his friend's bet. After all, how many times has he reminded me so far that he's competitive? It's how we wound up in this situation in the first place. Because he couldn't stand the idea of losing one silly bet with a friend.

Still, this seems like more lengths

than he has to go to just to win.

Breakfast in bed, complimenting me,

reminding me of how well we know

each other, how this is more than just

a weekend fling. He knows me, and I

know him too.

Could this be real?

He catches me watching him and

smiles at me, lifting his cup of coffee

in salute. I lift mine too, and we share

a smile, before we both take slow

drinks, our eyes never leaving one

another's. I want to know. I want to

ask him if this is real. But I don't,

because I'm scared.

What if he says no? What if he

thinks I'm crazy for reading more into

this than there really is? He told me

upfront that this was just a one

weekend deal, one silly bet, and then

it would be over.

I can't fall for him. Not anymore

than I already have. It's bad enough I

let myself get embroiled this deep. We

only have one day and one night left here. I'll enjoy it, and then come tomorrow, I'll take this ring off my finger and stop being his wife.

This is the only time we'll ever get together.

As much as it hurts to think about, I know I'm making the smart choice. Better this than risking getting my heart broken.

CHAPTER TEN

After breakfast in bed, we head down
to the spa to meet Meghan and Paul.
They're smiling, chatty. If they heard
us screaming in our room all night
long, they don't let on. They greet us
with hugs and then Meghan hooks her
arm through mine and points to the
spa features.

"Looks like the massage rooms are separated by gender," she explains, "And there's a free facial package we should probably take advantage of too. We can meet the boys afterward in the steam room and sauna, those are connected for both men and women. You fine with me kidnapping your wife for a bit, Luke?" she calls over her shoulder, probably because he's been trailing us from the moment we walked away, his gaze fixed on me.

I flash him a grin as he chuckles. "Just keep in mind, I'm a jealous husband," he tells Meghan with a wink.

"I promise to bring her back in one piece," Meghan calls. Then we duck into the massage room.

Unbeknownst to me, apparently Luke booked ahead for all four of us. At any rate, the spa attendants seem to recognize us at once and they lead us into a joint room, where they have us lie face down on tables and oil up our backs. It is quite possibly the best massage I've ever had—and a desperately needed one after last night's marathon workout sex. Every muscle in my body feels sore, in ways I never knew were possible. So it feels fantastic to have them knead out the knots now, even if it keeps making me groan in pain.

"Worked out recently?" Meghan

asks, with a knowing smirk.

"Something like that," I admit, my cheeks flushed bright red as I think about how much noise we made last night. Not to mention what we did in the hot tub. I wonder if Meghan and Paul noticed us, from where they were on the dance floor.

"I'm sure." She laughs. "So tell me, is Luke as great in bed as he looks like he'd be?"

My cheeks flush even worse than

before. "Er, well... I mean..."

"Because damn, that man is attractive as hell," she adds with an almost wistful sigh.

Something unpleasant curls in my stomach for a moment. *He's not mine*, I tell myself. *I can't act jealous if I'm not even really his wife.* Still. "That *is* why I married him, after all," I say a little testily. Then I catch myself. "One of the reasons, I mean. Also for his brain. And his personality. And, well..."

Meghan laughs, sounding lighthearted. "Relax, Celia, I'm only teasing. Besides, I think you're smoking hot too, y'know." She reaches over to nudge my shoulder with one hand, and my face, if anything, blushes worse than ever.

"Thanks. You're hot too," I add, because it seems like the polite thing to say, and because, well, she is. She and Paul both are. "You guys make a gorgeous couple."

"Thanks." Meghan sighs happily. "Is it crazy that I'm actually looking *forward* to being married?"

I glance over and catch her studying her engagement ring with a contended smile. I find myself watching her more closely, feeling a fresh bloom of jealousy now for an entirely different reason. "Of course not. I think that makes perfect sense. You found the right guy to settle down with, and now you're going to be with him for the rest of your lives. Why

wouldn't that be something to look

forward to?"

"You just hear so many people

talking about settling down as... well,

settling. As putting on the old ball and

chain and never having any more fun.

I don't think it's going to be like that

for us. Paul and I are still going to have

fun, and neither of us are *settling* for

each other."

"Of course not," I agree. "It's not

settling if you're both head over heels in love." I catch myself looking at my own ring too, turning it this way and that to enjoy the way the diamond catches the lights in here, reflecting them back in dozens of multicolored sparkles that dance along the walls. When the masseuse nudges me to turn over for the facial, I roll onto my back and rest both hands on my stomach, my right one over my left, toying with the ring absently as I think about how nice that must be. To feel certain about your partner. To know you are marrying for the right reasons, and the right person.

To know exactly how you both feel, and to be certain you are on the same page about it.

Yes, I am jealous of Meghan, but not because she thinks Luke is hot. It's because she's got a normal engagement, leading up to a real marriage, and me? I just have this weekend. I just have a couple days of playing pretend, and then it'll be back to the real world.

"Hey." Meghan's hand brushes my shoulder again. "You okay?"

I glance over at her, and then do I realize that a tear escaped my eye and tracked its way down my cheek. I wipe it away, feeling more embarrassed than ever, my face white hot now. "Yeah, fine," I mumble, my voice thick and unconvincing. "Just, um... something in my eye. Lotion or oil or something."

Her hand drops away, and she lies back on her spa bed, closing her eyes. If she doesn't believe me, at least she's nice enough not to call me out on it.

I shut my eyes too, and try to relax back into the spa treatment, instead of letting my brain run in circles worrying what's going to happen when this weekend ends.

CHAPTER ELEVEN

We head out to meet the guys in the

sauna area, our bodies loose and

relaxed from the massages, and my

face feeling soft and smooth from the

moisturizers they piled onto it after

the facial. I breathe in a sigh of

contentment as I step out of the

massage room and into the main area

of the spa. The air is a little cooler out here, probably to provide a contrast between the different saunas and steam rooms.

Meghan taps my shoulder. "I've got to run to the restroom. Why don't you figure out which sauna the guys are in and I'll catch up to you?"

I flash her a thumbs up and turn to study the different chambers. There's a few of them: a big stone chamber that looks like an oven, with a wood fire burning inside it. Another with what look like jade crystals embedded into the walls all around it, also with wood smoke. Then there are a couple of steam baths, small eight or ten-person sized bubbles filled with so much steam you can barely see inside the windows.

I check the two saunas first and find them empty. Then I open the door to the first steam room. The scent of eucalyptus and mint spills out, along with the sound of voices.

"—two weeks until the wedding," Paul is saying. "We just wanted to have our last fun as... well, you know. As a non-married couple."

"Define fun, exactly." Luke's voice sounds funny, constricted a little. Almost... angry? But that can't be right.

"You know. A little sharing, a little mutual pleasure. I mean, we heard you guys last night, and it definitely sounded like a fantastic time."

My cheeks flush, not from the steam either. *Is Paul suggesting what I think he is?* I think back to Meghan's comments in the massage room. *Besides, I think you're smoking hot too*. Was this what she meant? That she wanted to... what, *share* me with her husband? And Luke?

I hesitate, holding my breath. *What is Luke going to say?* On the one hand, Paul and Meghan are very attractive. But on the other, I'm not sure I'm into the idea of sharing Luke.

Not when I finally get to have him all

to myself, after all this waiting. I can't

stand the idea of seeing him with

Meghan. It turns my stomach, even if I

know she only meant it in fun.

"Absolutely not," Luke says, and I

let my breath out in a rush, relieved.

Paul laughs a little, though it

sounds weak. "I didn't mean anything,

man. I only thought the four of us

could have some fun together. Celia's

extremely hot, you clearly hit the

jackpot, and I'd say I did too, although

I might be biased... Why not share the

wealth a little, you know?"

"Because I'm greedy," Luke

responds without missing a beat.

"While I agree with you—she *is*

amazing—I'd never share Celia. Not

with *anyone*."

There's a tense silence, but I

don't even notice, because I'm too

busy feeling a rush of relief. I realize

I've been standing in the doorway,

letting the heat and steam out of the

room, and I step inside fully, pulling

the door shut behind me. I step over

to the bench where the boys are

sitting just in time to witness them

hugging, Luke slapping his friend's

back.

"Sorry, man, I'm sorry, that was

out of line," Paul is saying.

"Don't worry about it," Luke says,

and then his eyes flash to mine. "Celia.

How did spa day go?"

"Great," I say, unable to keep the stupid, wide grin off my face at hearing him defend me like that, when he didn't even realize I could hear him. *I'd never share Celia. Never*, he said. Not just "not for this weekend." I can hardly breathe; my head is spinning from so much happiness—not to mention from the steam is here.

I plop down next to Luke and rest a hand on his thigh, and he immediately wraps an arm around my shoulders, protective and comforting all at once. "How was your guys' day so far?"

"Massages were excellent," he says. "The steam room, I'm not so sure about."

Paul leans around him to nod. "You know, I think the steam is getting to my head, actually. I'm going to go pop out for a minute, try and clear it."

Luke relaxes the moment his

friend leaves, holding me closer

against his side. I snuggle into him,

unable to repress my smile any

longer, and rest my head on his

shoulder. "I kind of like it in here," I

say, and I can hear the smile in his

voice when Luke says, "Me too. Now,

anyway."

CHAPTER TWELVE

At sunset, we join the hotel crowd on the beach just below the cliffs where the building sits. There's a huge bonfire already going by the time we get there, since after sundown it tends to get a bit chilly on the waterfront. The sun hasn't set quite yet, but it's starting to turn orange, and painting the wisps of clouds along the horizon bright pink as it goes.

The hotel bar sent down a cart to set up, along with a bartender and beach themed cocktails. I order a piña colada inside an actual coconut. Meghan and Paul toast us with theirs, and the four of us walk down to the water to dip our toes in. As usual, the Pacific's water is frigid, but it's a nice shock to the system, especially after the walk across the hot white sand.

We chat and smile, until Meghan complains that her feet are getting too cold. She and Paul promise to save us a spot near the fire, and they head back up, leaving me and Luke alone with the lapping waves. We walk back a few paces from the water's edge, and he spreads out the jacket he brought with him for me to sit on. He just sits straight down on the sand himself.

"It is beautiful here," I say,

sipping my drink. He takes a long

drink of his and nods.

"It is," he says, but his eyes never

leave my face. He doesn't even seem

to notice the setting sun or the beach

around us. Nothing but me. It makes a

curl of pleasure swirl through my

body. I can't help it. I start to smile,

broad and unstoppable.

His words from earlier have

been stuck in my head all day. *I'd never*

share Celia. Does that mean what I

think it does? That there really is something between us, that this whole thing is real. Luke isn't just playing around—or maybe he started out playing around, on account of the silly bet. But now he isn't. I know it, just as suddenly and surely as I know that what I feel for him is more than just a silly office crush, too.

We know each other. We get along and have for a year. And now, we both know there's more to it than just flirtation. There's real chemistry

here, and real feelings, too.

He leans in to kiss me, and my

toes curl in the sand, even as I slide

one hand up to bury it in his hair. This

time his kiss is soft and slow and

sweet. So tender it makes my heart

ache with want. When we break apart,

both our faces are flushed, even

redder than the setting sun is

currently painting them.

We linger like that, foreheads

pressed together, gazes locked, as the sun dips below the horizon. All around us on the beach, we hear people cheering for the sunset. But it almost feels like they're cheering for us, like this moment is a little slice of what our life together could be like, if we made this more than just a one weekend affair.

It makes my head swim with happiness. It makes me want *more*. And I think Luke does too.

"This weekend…" He hesitates. Tries again. "Celia, I can't tell you enough how much I appreciate everything about you."

I smile at him, cupping his cheek. "Isn't that what wives are for?"

He smiles back and tilts his head to one side to plant a slow kiss right in the center of my palm. "I just hope I've been a good enough husband to make up for it."

"Oh, more than enough." I trail

my hand down to his chest, and let my palm rest there, feeling his slow, steady heartbeat. "I could get used to this," I whisper.

But between the wind and the waves, I'm not sure I spoke loud enough for him to hear me. His gaze has drifted away from mine, out over the waves, like he's considering the newly set sun and the pink painted wisps of cloud that still hover just above the horizon.

We sit in companionable silence for a few minutes, until I notice his drink is empty. Gently, I disentangle it from his fingers. He sees what I'm doing and moves to stand. "Let me," he says. "Do you need another?"

But I shake my head, already halfway to my feet. "I'll go. Same again?" I wiggle his empty beer, and he nods. Unable to hide my smile, which feels stupidly wide, stretching practically from ear to ear, I jog back across the sand toward the bar set up, my heart fizzing with happiness.

This weekend is the start of something. I just know it is.

When I finally reach the bar, Paul is already in line there. I look around for Meghan and find her chatting to some girls near the firepit, waving her drink around to demonstrate some point. Paul waves and smiles as I approach. "Luke sending you on drink duty?" He shakes his head and *tsks*.

"What a lazy husband you've got."

I snort. "Nah, I volunteered for this one. Needed to stretch my legs." I fall into line behind him after depositing my empty glasses on the bar. I feel awkward for a moment, aware of Paul's eyes on me, and remembering his comments earlier. But he apologized to Luke already, and he didn't mean anything bad I'm sure. He just wanted a foursome, that's all.

Still, it makes my cheeks flame

thinking about it, especially now that we're alone in line. But it also reminds me that I owe Paul. After all, without him, none of this would have happened.

I check over my shoulder. Meghan still seems engaged in her conversation. I remember how the guys didn't discuss the bet in front of her and think I should probably stick to that. But for now, since it's just me and Paul... "Hey, I owe you a thank you, Paul."

He glances at me, eyebrows lifted in confusion. "Oh? What do you mean?"

"Well, if it wasn't for your and Luke's little bet, I don't know that I ever would have wound up here with him." I glance down at the ring sparkling on my finger, aware that I need to tread carefully. I can't let him know we only *pretended* to get married for the bet. But if he thinks that's why we moved things along a little more quickly, well...

But when I glance back up, I find Paul frowning at me in the dimming evening light. "What bet are you talking about?"

"You know." I wiggle my wedding ring. It sparkles in the distant bonfire light. "When you two bet on which one of you would get married first?" He opens his mouth, but I hold up a hand to stave him off. "Now, I'm not saying

Luke and I wouldn't have gotten married otherwise, of course. Just, I think having that bet in the back of his mind made him a little more open to the idea. We probably wouldn't have gotten as close to one another as quickly as we did, otherwise." Even if it did still take a whole year of me mooning after him at work for him to notice.

But Paul is still frowning at me, eyebrows knit in confusion. "I don't know what you're talking about, Celia,"

he says slowly, as though I'm the one

acting crazy.

It sinks in, little by little. Slow

enough that I feel crazy too, gaping at

him as my mind whirs. "You mean…" I

clear my throat. "You and Luke never,

um… never bet that you'd get married

before the other one?"

He shakes his head. "No. Sorry,

Celia. Maybe you're confusing me with

another of his friends?"

But I'm not. I *know* I'm not. It's the whole reason Luke invited me on this weekend. The whole reason he's had me pretending to be his wife this whole time. It was all because Paul was here. At least, so he claimed.

What is going on?

CHAPTER THIRTEEN

I leave the drinks line, unable to pretend everything is normal. Vaguely, behind me, I can hear Paul calling out after me, asking if I'm okay. I just wave and shout over my shoulder that I'll be right back.

I won't be, though.

I stumble blindly through the

sand, tears stinging at the backs of my eyes. *Luke lied to me?* This whole time, he's had me acting up a storm, all for some bet he claimed he had. If that didn't exist... why did he do all of this? Why bring me here?

Was he trying to get me to make a fool out of myself? Trying to push me, to see how far I'd let him go? Was he just taking advantage of me, the dumb office secretary who clearly had a huge crush on her boss?

I can hardly see anything; my eyes have blurred so much. I stumble along the beach wiping at them with my palms, but it doesn't do any good. The tears just keep coming, as I imagine every terrible reason Luke could have for tricking me into doing this.

I hear footsteps, and I whirl around. I recognize the silhouette of the figure jogging toward me immediately. He's impossible to mistake, even in the falling dark, even

out on this dimly lit beach. "Go away," I

shout, before Luke has even reached

my side.

I whirl back around and continue

to stagger away. But it's getting darker,

and I can't always see the dips and

hollows in the shifting sand. I stumble,

and almost fall, before I feel warm

hands close around my arm and haul

me back upright.

I brush Luke off with an effort. "I

don't want to talk to you."

"Celia…"

I wrench my arm free from his grip and whirl on him instead. "Have you just been playing games with me? This whole time, has it just been one big mind game to you?"

He stares at me for a long moment, eyes inscrutable in the dark. Finally, he sighs. "You must have figured things out."

Tears start to track down my

cheeks. I'm powerless to stop them,

no matter how much I hate to cry in

front of him now. I rub at my eyes, my

voice choked. "How could you lie to

me like this? What were you trying to

do, just humiliate me, see how much

I'd do for you?"

"No, Celia, that's not it at all." He

reaches for me again, and this time I

don't have the energy to push him off

or back away. I let him wrap his hands

around my shoulders, strong and

steadying. Even now, furious as I am at

him, his touch feels reassuring, safe

somehow. It makes me angrier than

ever, knowing he still has that effect

on me, even though he shouldn't.

"Then explain it to me," I

whisper, tilting my head up so I can

see as much of his face as possible in

the dim light.

He reaches one hand up to

brush stray strands of hair back from

my forehead. The wind is stronger

down here on the beach, and it's

worked its wildness into my hair,

blowing it every which way as I ran up

the beach away from the party. Away

from everyone. Away from *him*. When

he's finished brushing my hair back,

he leaves his hand cupped against my

cheek. His thumb catches a stray tear,

and he brushes it away. "Celia, I..." He

takes a deep breath. "I found your

fanfiction."

Whatever I thought he was

about to say, it wasn't that. My heart sinks straight through my stomach and into the ground. "Oh, no..." I start to back away, but he tightens his grasp on me.

"No, it's okay. It was my fault. I was working late one night, and I was trying to find something I emailed to you, but I accidentally deleted it from my sent folder. I turned on your monitor thinking I could just grab it from your recent messages, and the fanfiction was open on your screen."

He winces a little, teeth a flash of white in the growing starlight. "I shouldn't have snooped, I know that. But once I started reading, I couldn't stop. Celia, you're a *really* good writer."

I laugh, and it comes out choked and teary.

"Not to mention, you have a dirty as hell mind." He smirks.

I manage a watery smile in return.

"From the moment you first walked into my office, I had a crush on you," he says, and my heart leaps back out of the floor into my chest with a thud. "I didn't think you were interested in me in the same way, though. I never saw any indication from you of anything like that."

My jaw drops open. *He liked me? All along he liked me?*

"I... I started following your account. On the fanfic site where you write. I'd read every new thing you posted."

Now my face flares hot again, as embarrassment floods me. *Oh God.* I would have written things differently if I'd known he was reading. But then... isn't it better I didn't edit myself? That he knows what my deepest fantasies are now? "Did... did you...?"

"Jerk off to them?" He lifts an eyebrow. "Oh hell yes, Celia. All the damn time. The things you'd imagine me doing to you... *Fuck,* I wanted those stories to be real. I wanted to do all those things to you and more."

My lips part just a little in shock, as I study him in the dark. "But you never said," I whisper.

"I'm your boss," he points out. "I couldn't exactly just make a move on you. It wouldn't have been proper." He cocks his head to one side, and I can feel rather than see the way his eyebrow must be lifted in sarcasm right now. "And I also knew, with equal certainty, that you were too shy to ever make a move on your own. Weren't you?"

I swallow hard and let out a slow sigh. "Probably." I did spend an entire year just wasting away in fantasy land after all, didn't I?

"So..." He shrugs, and spreads his hands wide, gesturing around us. At the beach, the waves. The falling night, the distant bonfire and music. The hotel on the cliff high above us here.

Everything. "I thought if I could

convince you to spend time with me

outside of work, with a good enough

excuse for why you didn't need to stick

to the rules of office propriety

anymore, then maybe that dirty girl

from your fantasies would come out

to play." He steps closer, until he's just

an inch away from me, warm heat

radiating from his chest, from his arms

where they encircle me. "I thought

maybe you'd relax this weekend.

Come out of your shell." His smile

deepens. "Come in general, a lot."

I huff out another laugh, this one

much breathier than the first.

"Was I wrong?" he asks, head

tilted to one side.

I suck in a deep breath. My tears

are gone, replaced by... well. So many

feelings I'm not even sure which ones

to focus on. Happiness. *Giddiness,*

really. But he still lied to me. He still

manipulated me, even if it was to get me to come out of the shy shell I have myself constantly trapped inside.

"Are you mad?" he whispers, his breath soft on my cheeks.

"Mad?" I repeat. I gently break free from his arms. He lets them fall to his sides, limp with worry. "Mad?" I repeat, taking a few steps to one side, toward where the ocean waves have begun to encroach on our spot. Without any more warning, I kick at the water, sending a wave of it

cascading onto his body. "Of course

I'm mad!" I yell, laughing. Then I run at

him, while he's still wiping the salt

water from his face. I grab his face in

both my hands and pull him, both of

us laughing, down into a hard, deep

kiss. "I'm furious at you for lying to

me," I whisper, once our lips part

again. "That's no way to treat

someone you care about. But..." I

hesitate. Lick my lips. "This was also

the best weekend I've ever had." I

search his eyes. "It's been like living in

a dream..." I swallow around the lump

of embarrassment in my throat. "It's

been like one of my fantasies come to

life." I tilt my head, studying him. "Until

now."

He cups my cheek. "The dream

doesn't have to end, Celia," he

whispers. "Not now... not ever." Then

he leans in to kiss me again, slower

this time, and I taste salt on his lips,

heat on his tongue. We break apart,

and he's smiling, huge and real. "I love

you, Celia," he says, and everything in

me lights up, like fireworks going off.

I wrap my arms around his neck

and let him lift me off my feet.

CHAPTER FOURTEEN

I don't even remember how we found

the cave. I just remember running

across the sand, my hand in Luke's.

Every few feet he'd stop and pick me

up and whirl me around, kissing me,

before he'd set me back down again to

run some more. When we finally

stumble across the cave, set deep into

the cliff face, we can't even hear the

music down the beach anymore, or

the crackle of the bonfire. There's just

the slow, steady crash of the waves,

and the whisper of the wind between

the rocks over our heads.

He spreads out his coat again,

and this time he's the one who sits

down, right before he pulls me onto

his lap, holding one of my thighs to

each side of his waist so I'm straddling

him, my hike splayed over his lap. He

wraps strong hands around my waist

and draws my hips down against his, until I can feel the hard throb of his cock beneath me.

"I love you, Celia," he repeats, and it feels more meaningful than ever now, everything we've done, all the sex we've had.

I arch my hips against him, dragging my crotch against his, savoring the hard press of his cock against my pussy, through the fabric of my panties. "I love you, Luke," I whisper back, just like I have a million times before in my head, in my fantasies of this moment.

It feels so much better in real life than it ever could have in my imagination.

He uses his thumbs to hook under my panties and tug them down. I reach down to push off his pants at the same time, and it doesn't take long before we're naked again, skin to skin, me poised over him on the sand. He guides me toward him, until I feel the

press of his cock against my lower lips,

and then between them.

"I love you," he repeats, just as

the tip of his cock finds my entrance

and presses inside. I let out a little

half-moan of pleasure and sink lower

against him, lowering myself onto his

cock inch by inch.

"I love you," I whisper back, once

he's fully inside me, every inch of him

filling me up, stretching me, making

me feel full. My pussy aches from last night still, but it's a pleasant, bone deep ache. The kind that only makes me want more.

But it's different this time. He guides me, setting the pace, and we move together slowly, sweetly. It's not a searing hot, rough wildfire like our sex has been before. It's a slow build. He holds me tight against his chest, so I feel every inch of our bodies pressed together, his naked skin against mine, his cock buried deep inside me. He drops one hand between us to run his thumb gently across my mound, before dipping it lower to graze my clit, until I gasp.

He smiles, watching me. "So fucking sexy," he whispers, as he strokes me, gently at first, then a little faster, enough to make my head fall back as I arch my back into him, nearing a peak. "God, I love watching you come, Celia," he murmurs, even as

I let myself go, let the orgasm sweep me away for a second, rushing through my whole body.

He keeps going the whole time, gently rocking up into me, slow and steady until neither of us can stand it anymore. "I want to feel you come," I murmur. "I want to feel your cum inside me, Luke."

He obeys me this time, tightening his grip on my hips and speeding up his thrusts until he's driving up into me, again and again,

until I can feel the shudder building in

him. When he comes, I pull him

against me, kissing him hard to muffle

his groan. I feel it in every inch of his

body, the pleasure, the release. The

way he breaks apart to gaze at me

with awe, like I'm some kind of

magical, beautiful creature who he

can't quite believe is with him right

now.

I know the feeling. I slide off his

lap, and we lie side by side on the

sand, face to face, on top of his coat.

He traces my lower lip with his thumb.

I reach up to run my fingertips along

the sides of his face, his jawline, the

edges of his lips.

"Did you mean it?" I whisper,

eventually.

"Did I mean that I love you?" he

responds, reaching up to pull me

against him more tightly. His lips find

my temple, my cheek, my jawline. He

nudges forward, kissing the spot

where my neck meets my jaw, and I

gasp a little before I sink into him,

surrendering.

"No," I breathe, trying to keep my

heart rate steady, my breath from

hitching. "Did you mean it... when you

said that the dream doesn't have to

end?"

He pulls back, and I freeze,

worried I've done something wrong.

He shifts me off him and stands, and

then he wraps both hands around

mine and tugs me to my feet.

"What are you doing?" I ask, but

he doesn't answer me. He just takes

my left hand in his, ever so gently.

"Can I have the ring back, Celia?"

My heart sinks. So, *no*, he meant.

He didn't mean it. The fantasy does

have to end. Trying to ignore the sting

in the back of my throat, I reach up

with shaking fingers and slide the ring

off my finger, before I pass it to him. I

hold my breath, unsure what he's

doing. Unsure what any of this means

now.

"I don't want you to be my wife

for now, Celia," Luke murmurs, and my

heart starts to stutter, to beat faster

with fear. But then he sinks down in

front of me, onto one knee in the

sand. He's still holding my left hand in

his—he never let me go. "I want you to

be my wife forever," he says, kneeling

in front of me, looking up at me in the

dim glow from the moon that's

starting to rise outside our little cave.

"Will you marry me for real, Celia?"

My eyes sting with fresh tears all

over again, but these are happy tears,

tears of joy. It takes me a moment to

find my voice. I just start nodding at

first, and he laughs, and then I laugh

too, and it all bursts out of me at once.

"Yes. Yes, Luke, I'll marry you for real."

He slides the ring back onto my finger

and stands, picking me up in his arms

and spinning me around, sand flying

around our feet.

He kisses me, again and again,

and I smile into the kiss, unable to

stop. When he finally sets me back on

my feet, we're both breathless,

laughing. I lift my hand and wiggle my

ring finger, studying the diamond in

the light.

"It feels heavier now," I observe.

"Like it really means something this

time."

When I glance over, I find him studying me closely, through hooded eyes. I recognize that look. It's the look he gets when he wants me, so badly he can hardly stand it.

It's one of my favorite looks.

"That's because it does," he replies, taking a step toward me. He catches my hand and brings it to his lips, kissing the ring first, and then each of my fingertips in turn. "It's because this time, the ring was given with intention," he says, smiling. I smile back. I wonder if I'll ever stop doing that instinctively, smiling at him whenever he does. I hope not.

"I love you, Celia," he whispers. "I can't wait to be your husband for real."

THE END

Author Biography

Penny Wylder writes just that-- wild romances. Happily Ever Afters are always better when they're a little dirty, so if you're looking for a page turner that will make you feel naughty in all the right places, jump right in and leave your panties at the door!

Made in the USA
San Bernardino, CA
09 June 2019